Demolition man

New York Times Bestselling Author

max monroe

Dedication

To anyone who's ever had to fight like hell to
get to their happy ending.

And to ourselves—because this story *poured* out of us…and
very nearly killed us in the process.

Demolition man

CALLOWAY

MY PRESENCE IN THIS ROOM ALONE MAKES me feel complicit in an act so evil, it should earn a one-way ticket straight to hell.

A man I barely know sits beside me, watching from the corner of his eye as women are paraded across the room like products in a commercial.

It doesn't matter that this stranger calls himself my uncle.

It doesn't matter that his bringing me here may have saved my life.

What matters is the demeaning, objectifying, downright degrading scene that plays out in front of me.

Woman after woman in skimpy lingerie is brought through a door and guided onto a raised platform in the center. White numbers sit in front of them like lots in an estate sale.

Some smile and strut, while others do their best to maintain their composure under the bright, blinding lights.

I sit behind a one-way mirror alongside one hundred other male vampires waiting to place a bid on the woman of their choosing via an iPad system designed to maintain fairness and "order."

My skin crawls with discomfort and disgust, but to these men, *this* is normal.

Though, the real match strikes when *she* completes the line, stepping up to the left side of the platform and squinting into the light.

Auburn hair, black lingerie, and sweet cerulean eyes form a picture built for illicit temptation, met with the men's cruel indifference to the fear trembling through her body.

And when I see her hands shake, a silent scream begs for freedom from my throat.

She's not the only reason I'm doing this—far from it.

This is a moral imperative. A change to the way my fellow vampires live and the special relationship we have with humans. This is a reckoning for the good of the world and for the safety of women who've been used for years.

This is justice.

This is a revolution.

But she—Romy Spencer—makes it personal.

When I'm done with this place, every one of these monsters will beg for mercy while my brothers and I make sure they burn— no matter what it costs us.

1

ROMY

THE DULLNESS OF DISTRACTION GRAYS MY NOR-mally cerulean eyes in the big mirror of the Neiman Marcus bathroom as I wash my hands.

Outside the door, my mother waits impatiently to shop for my funeral.

"Romy! Hurry up," she commands, peeking her head in.

"Okay," I agree complacently before mumbling my dissent under my breath. "It's not like it's a normal bodily function to have to pee or anything."

Or like it's not outrageous that we're celebrating this shit anyway.

It's not that I'm afraid to stand up for myself—it's that I've been trying that to no avail for far too many years. Truly a futile endeavor at this point.

Snatching two paper towels from the holder and drying my hands, I sidle out of the bathroom with dread.

Of course, my mother has my elbow in hand before the door closes behind us, and we're on the move again.

We're closing in on hour three of shopping, and as of yet,

she's not happy with anything. It's too modest. Too slutty. Too polyester, too pink, too blue, too fricking *human*.

I tried reminding her that's what *we* are, but she wasn't thrilled with that brush with reality. For her, being called to this assignment is as close as you can get to nobility, and that requires a royal outfit befitting Princess Kate.

"You leave for New York *tonight*," she blathers, working herself into a fluster all over again with clout-chasing excitement. "If we don't find something here, I don't know what we'll do."

"Hey, I know!" I snap excitedly. "I'll just skip it. I'm too young to die anyway."

"Romy Spencer, stop it right now," she barks. "Stop complaining about this privilege and belittling the process that's been *very* important to our family for generations. And for the love of God, *stop* referring to it as your funeral. You're on my last nerve with that one." She lets out a long sigh. "Let's not forget that, despite my better judgment, I let you skip the Choosing Mixer."

Oh yeah. *The Choosing Mixer.* The big event where all the vampire men get to see what human women are on the menu.

When she turns to hurry down another aisle of high-slit-bearing dresses, I stick out my tongue behind her back.

I know it's an immature move for a woman in her early twenties—childish, even—but the whole context of the fight we're having calls for a little ridiculousness, if you ask me.

I mean, come *on*. In just five hours, I'm being shipped off from my home in Massachusetts to New York and *sold* to the highest bidder like a cow, all because my generationally passed-down blood is somehow valuable to a bunch of *vampires*.

And lucky for me, my family, the Spencers, are one of the last lines of blood belonging to the *blood of the three*—a powerful, biological makeup that somehow enhances the vampirical abilities of a whole secret group of paranormal or supernatural or *whatever* creatures that live among us.

Not to mention, I have one of only three human bloodlines in the world that vampires can reproduce with—not exactly an exciting scenario when you're about to be auctioned off to some unknown fangy man to have his fangy babies.

It's batshit *crazy*, and voluntary, but only in the sense that *everyone* is supposed to want to do it. Being that I'm an only child, the options in the family gene pool are limited—*aka me, myself, and I.*

And instead of shrieking in terror and plotting an escape plan worthy of James fucking Bond—like I would if *my* daughter had the special bloodline sauce—my mother is shopping for the perfect dress to market me in.

The snarky attitude, comparative remarks to my funeral, and juvenile tongue are the *least* I'm due.

"What about lavender?" my mother suggests, pulling a sequined, prom-like getup off the rack next to her. "It always goes so well with your blue eyes."

I sigh, and she returns the favor immediately, adding a frown to jazz it up. "Fine. No purple."

"It's not the purple, Mom. Please. This has nothing to do with the *color*, and you know it."

"Oh, I know, honey. You've made that abundantly clear. How *stupid* you think our family's legacy is. How beneath you the very idea of being *used* for your..." She lowers her voice to a whisper, ever so diligent about keeping the vampires' secrets like a good girl. "*Blood* is."

She shakes her head before turning back to the rack to flick through more dresses. "But this is more than that. This is a distinction and an honor given to a very select group of women that affects the very world as we know it. And you're not being used, Romy. You're being *selected*. You're being *chosen*. Those are very different things."

I suck my lips into my mouth, bracing for the speech she's given me a hundred different times in fifty different ways. *This isn't like jury duty, Romy. This is like winning the lottery.*

"It doesn't matter that the existence of vampires is a well-kept secret. Without them, the life you and I and everyone in this place knows…" She circles a finger next to her head in reference to the store and the town and the world, I guess. "…would be *very* different."

Some people worship God and Christ, but my mother skipped church and went straight to the elite vampires.

If it weren't all so tragic, I'd probably laugh. Or, at the very least, turn it into a comedy bit worthy of Netflix's attention.

"But you're selling me. You get that, right? That you're *selling* me?" I glare at her as my heart rate picks up speed inside my chest. "Some random-ass vampire with a lot of cash is going to decide I'm the blood and body and whatever else he's looking for, push the one-click button on the website, and pack me up to ship me off to his lair or whatever. It doesn't matter if I like him or his house or his breath smells. I'm freaking *sold.*"

"*Romy.*" She sighs again. "For far from the first time, it's an *endowment.* A gift, given both to the family and the Elite Council as a pledge of respect to the process and the woman they'll be bonding with. It's not eBay or Craigslist. It's a charitable contribution to the tradition. A symbol of the significance and a penance of gratitude." She sucks in a breath of frustration before continuing, "Your involvement is voluntary."

"*Clearly* not."

"Romy, please. We've been over this. You know this is what you have to do. You can't tell me you'd be better off with some *mechanic* from Amherst or something, for Pete's sake. These men are the best of the very best."

"Okay," I relent. It's not that I've changed my mind—it's that I know I won't change hers.

I've thought about running away and creating my own version of a new life before; I'm an adult, and this is a big world with a lot of possibilities, even when you're starting over.

Unfortunately, this isn't some human organization with incompetency issues and a quiet quitting epidemic. This is a group of highly attuned, highly sensitive, highly freaking gifted vampires who eat this kind of shit for breakfast. I know with every fiber of hatred I feel for this process that I'd be hunted down in no time at all and convinced to participate in ways that make this whole version of the shitshow seem like a walk in the park.

My mom and dad have spent way too many years waxing poetic about the power of the vampires and how intensely superior they are in practically every way for me to assume anything else. I'm no Lara Croft. My basic survival instincts and dependence on Wi-Fi would have me out of the game in a nanosecond.

No. I'm stuck here. Being sold to Vampire Island in New York—whether I damn well like it or not.

"Now, please, let's get back to it," my mother says, her relief obvious in the reappearance of her smile. "You need something that'll make you stand out."

"Got it."

New objective: find something that makes me blend in as much as humanly possible.

2

CAL

THREE BLUE-COLLAR VAMPIRES AND TWO HUMAN women in a cabin, and I'm the fifth wheel.

Rook has Kylie.

Kane has Blair.

Both of my brothers have found their fated mates. Meanwhile, I'm sitting at the kitchen table with a set of brake calipers pretending that counts as a personality.

I turn the metal over in my hands, cleaning parts that don't actually need cleaning, while the rest of the room carries on behind me.

Blair and Kylie are curled together on the couch whispering about something that makes them both laugh. The sound fills the cabin in a way that still feels strange after the past few weeks—light, normal, and the kind of peace we haven't had since this whole mess started.

Kane stands nearby, watching Blair like she's the only thing in existence, their fated mate bond practically humming in the air. Across the room, Rook leans against the wall, pretending not to listen while his mate Kylie elbows Blair and whispers something that sends them both into another round of laughter.

Even my eldest—and very much grumpiest—brother Rook looks relaxed. Honestly, that in itself is a miracle. Between the three of us, we've stacked enough bodies to get the vampire elite hunting us.

All in the name of saving Kylie and Blair.

The elites thought my brothers' fated mates were theirs to auction, claim, breed, and drain. Both of them are *blood of the three*—the most highly coveted human bloodlines by the vampire elite.

Obviously, we disagreed, and now the elite want us dead.

They already burned down our homes in Concordia. Destroyed my mechanic shop too. Every piece of the life we had before this mess is gone.

But they still haven't found this cabin—the little slice of serenity residing deep in unexplored forest that we built with our own bare hands.

It's our permanent home…for now. Or at least until we can figure out our next move.

Earlier today, I went with Kane and Blair so she could see her family in a quiet park outside Boston while I ran surveillance. If any of the elite's gofers had been anywhere near that place, I would've smelled them.

Blair's parents still think she's in New York with an elite vampire named Damien Snow.

The only problem with that story is Damien Snow is currently dead. Kane handled that personally.

Nonetheless, that lie is being fed to Blair's family by that slimefuck elite gofer Holland—the same bastard who tried to lure Kylie into the elites' little viper nest and drugged Blair to deliver her to Damien's penthouse.

Honestly, I'd love to rip Holland's head off myself, but I'm pretty sure Kane and Rook would fight me for the privilege.

When Blair finished talking to her parents today, she made a choice to continue to keep them in the dark to protect them. Which means her family still believes she's being courted by an elite.

They have no idea she's hiding out in a cabin with three blue-collar vampires the elite want dead.

And somehow, despite everything, tonight actually feels calm.

Kane glances at Blair. She catches him staring and rolls her eyes like she's already exhausted by his existence. But she also smiles too.

Of course Kane grins like a damn idiot. I swear, their version of foreplay is something I'll never understand.

I shake my head and return my attention to the caliper in my hands, though most of my focus isn't actually on the metal. Part of my brain stays locked on the outside world at all times—tracking distant engines on the highway miles away, the wind moving through the trees, the occasional rustle of animals in the woods. Super hearing—it's my power—is great when you're trying to stay alive, but it also means peace is mostly an illusion.

Still, for the first time since this whole mess started, my brothers actually look happy.

Which is probably why the knock on the door feels like someone dropped a grenade in the middle of the room.

The sound cracks through the cabin, and everyone freezes.

Rook looks up, and I'm already on my feet, while Kane follows my lead to the front door.

No one ever comes to this cabin. Besides us, no one should know it's here.

A second knock follows the first, and my senses sharpen automatically. I listen past the wood and glass, searching for the familiar chaos of multiple heartbeats or footsteps or weapons shifting.

But there's only *one* set of footsteps.

Both of my brothers glance over their shoulders to make sure Blair and Kylie are still on the couch, and concern is clear on both women's faces.

Without a word, Rook and I move closer to the door with Kane. Three brothers in one line, shielding the women behind us.

Rook pulls the door open, and one singular man stands on the porch.

He's tall, expensively dressed, and has pepper-gray hair combed neatly back. His glowing green eyes move slowly across the three of us, like he has all the time in the world and we're just the people he's been looking for.

And he's smiling with the confidence of a man who believes he's untouchable in a way that only a very old, very powerful elite vampire would.

Because that's exactly what he is.

It's written all over his face. It emanates from his fucking royal blood. And it's showcased in every inch of his expensive but completely-impractical-for-being-in-the-fucking-forest wardrobe.

"Hello, Rook. Kane." His smile deepens as his eyes slide to me and flare slightly. "Calloway."

A cold weight settles in my chest. He knows our names, but we don't fucking know him.

"Who the fuck are you?" Rook asks without hesitation.

The man laughs, a full, amused sound that rumbles in his chest as his gaze moves slowly across us again—first Kane, then Rook, then me. "Lucian," he declares. "Lucian Wrath. Vice President of the Elite Council."

Fuck. They found us.

Something strange flickers across his face—not hostility, not approval, but something else entirely. Whatever it is, it sets every instinct in my body on edge.

"I've been waiting for this moment," Lucian adds quietly.

The words hang in the night air.

His gaze drifts past us toward the inside of the cabin before returning to our faces. "I knew you three would be the ones to change things."

Lucian Wrath's smile isn't of the happy variety—it's fucking *ominous*—and then, with two fingers to his lips, he lets out a low whistle from his mouth. The sound barely leaves his throat before the night explodes into chaos.

Men in black cars screech to a stop in the driveway and move more quickly than we can react to surround the house.

We're fast, but so are they—because they're vampires too. I recognize the sharp jaws and superior physiques, but even if I didn't, they're the ones we've been expecting.

This war we started is in full swing. The men we've killed demand to be avenged. The women we've taken—though bound to Slaters by the universe's decree—they believe were promised to them.

By their code, we owe them our heads. This isn't a slap on the wrist. This is high treason. Traitorhood. The worst betrayal possible.

If anything, I'm only surprised they didn't find us sooner.

"Shit, Kane. Guard the back door. Now," I command, desperate to put up some line of defense as we're outnumbered at least three to one. But it's too late. Men are in the house, in the back hall, and barging through the front door as we speak.

Kylie screams.

Blair cries out for Kane.

And as the only one of us with less to lose, I step in front of my brothers and their mates and ready myself for a fight. I'll die if I have to—but they won't. Their mates won't.

I refuse to let that happen.

I'm on the first man quickly, taking him by surprise as I force him to the floor and put my knee to his neck, ready to break it. Blair screams, but before I can execute, I'm stopped by a blinding light in my eyes and a pulsing pain in my chest.

Fuuuuuck!

I'm not just weak—I'm practically paralyzed.

"Cal!" Kane shouts, charging toward me until he's forced to hit his knees as well.

"Don't!" I croak, trying to warn Rook as he tenses with offense.

The pain is all-consuming, and I look down at my limbs to make sure they aren't being ripped from my body. Kane isn't any better—he's on the floor beside me, his jaw clenched and a vein popping from the center of his forehead.

"Kane! Oh my God, Kane!" Blair screams for him again.

"No, baby!" Kane says through gritted teeth. "Stay there, Blair!"

The pain rips through every cell in my body as Lucian casually moves toward me, nonchalantly stepping over the vamp I just took to the floor.

I scuttle back, trying to put distance between us, but he just stands there looking down at Kane, adjusting the sleeves of his black suit jacket with a smile.

In the light of the cabin, I can see him more clearly now and, though older, his features are still bright and sharp with youth. His green eyes radiate, and I know instantly that he's the one responsible for our current pain.

"Stop!" Rook demands from behind me, his bark almost as fucking intimidating as his bite.

Lucian's smile only deepens.

"Don't, Rook!" I croak, holding the weight in my chest with all the strength I have. It feels like it could smother me—and I don't even need fucking air.

Yep. We're fucked.

Eventually, though, Lucian sighs. "But perhaps, more appropriate for this occasion…" He pauses and looks around the room at the vampires who are prepared to finish us off. "Gentlemen, please. If you'd leave us for a moment?"

They all retreat quickly, obviously at Lucian's discretion for orders. I don't know if they're gofers or protection detail, but I can tell from the way my chest fucking cracks, this fucker doesn't need either to get his point across.

As the last of the guys leaves the room, a vampire the size

of a bear knocks a picture frame of the three of us as kids off the wall. It shatters when it hits the hardwood floor.

Lucian sighs again, and before I know it, the man is across the room with his throat in Lucian's hand. "What did I say about unnecessary childishness, Lexor?"

"I'm sorry, Lucian," the big fucker rushes to apologize. "I'm sorry!"

But sorry isn't good enough, and in a matter of half a second, he's no more than a pile of bones on the floor.

Both Blair and Kylie gasp behind me.

"Sorry, ladies," Lucian says, dusting off his hands and stepping over what used to be Lexor, and then he waves a lazy hand toward Kane and me.

Instantly, the pain releases its choke hold on my body.

Both Kane and I struggle to get to our feet, and Blair rushes over to him before he can stop her. He wraps his arm around her shoulder protectively, and I don't hesitate to meet the vice president of the Elite Council with every bit of aggression he deserves.

"All right, *Lucian Wrath*. We get it. You're more powerful than we can even imagine. You've had your fun showing off, so let's get down to business. What's going to happen to us?"

He nods, a shine of pride radiating from his eyes. "Oh, Calloway. I knew you'd be tough. Your mother was strong too."

"You knew our mother?" Kane asks, his voice sounding far more boyish than it ever has.

Lucian nods. "Of course. I'm your uncle."

What the fuck? My body sways at the news.

Lucian Wrath, an *elite* vampire, is the uncle to three *blue-collar* ones. It doesn't make sense. That's not how any of this works. Blue-collars and elites don't stem from the same bloodlines.

"No…" I shake my head. "You can't be."

"Yes, yes." He smiles at me. "You have good reason to think that. But I assure you, I *am*. My brothers…discarded you, but you are of their flesh and blood. You are elites. All three of you."

"Fuck that," Rook declares, Kylie tucked tightly behind him now. "We don't want it. We're fine just as we are."

And neither Kane nor I go against him.

Maybe other blue-collar vampires would want a piece of the elite pie, but not us. We want nothing to do with these disgusting fucks—no matter if they just-so-happen to be family or not. Frankly, the fact that we are related to such a perverse group of vampires only leaves a bitter fucking taste on my tongue.

Lucian nods, his expression a picture of performative understanding. "I sympathize with your rejection, Rook. Truly. After the life you've lived, this news can feel like nothing more than spit in the face." He wags a finger and tilts his jaw. "However, given the recent…activities…you and your brothers have partaken in, and the nature of their punishment, I'm afraid the reality of your bloodline is of utmost importance. It's why *I've* come myself. To help you."

Fucking bullshit. To track us down and come *here*, to our secret, off-the-grid cabin in Connecticut, claiming to be our family, and purporting himself as some kind of savior in this scenario is the height of irony.

It's men like him who've brought us here—who've forced Rook, Kane, and me into taking things into our hands and going against their vicious practices of selling women to the highest bidder. Of going against their hoarding of bloodlines in the name of power and longevity and greed.

He's not a hero. He's a fucking sadist.

My body prepares to strike—consequences be damned.

"Now, now, Calloway, put away your fangs, my boy," Lucian comments with a disappointed smirk. "This isn't the time for that."

"I'm not your boy, *uncle*," I seethe, prompting a growl from Rook behind me.

Instantly, two black-cloaked vampires bang on the back door, sensing the escalation of tension, but Lucian holds up a hand and the noise stops.

"Cal," Kane murmurs, urgency and desperation in his voice setting my teeth on edge. It's not fear, but a willingness to do literally anything to protect his fated mate.

I don't understand the total capacity of the mating bond yet, at least not fully, and for that, I'm both thankful and annoyed.

Truth be told, Kane shouldn't have been capable of meeting his mate yet. Biologically, a male vampire isn't supposed to be able to recognize the bond until we hit the ripe age of twenty-eight. That's when we come fully into our vampirehood. It's when we begin to fully recognize any powers we may possess and the aging process becomes nearly five times slower than a human.

But Kane is only twenty-seven. And I'm twenty-six. Rook is the only twenty-eight-year-old vampire out of our trio who should be capable of finding his destined mate.

"Listen, boys," Lucian says teasingly, using the simple moniker to knock us down a peg. "This doesn't have to be so tense. I'm here with good news. You're of noble blood. You're elites. That means all this…mess…you've created is far less consequential than it could be."

"Nothing about your little visit screams good news," Rook insists, taking the words right out of my own mouth. "We don't do well with ultimatums, threats, or intimidation tactics."

"What threats?" He retorts with an infuriating chuckle. "I'm simply executing a reunion that should have happened a long time ago." His voice takes on a lilt. "Oh, how I wish we could have done it sooner than this, but it's better late than never. And quite frankly, very poetic in its timing. I'm inviting you to take a very distinguished place at your rightful station in New York, just in time for the selection process. I know your brothers have mated, but Cal, you will have the first Slater chance at choosing for yourself."

Selection process? You have got to be kidding me. I'd rather cut off my dick than be involved in their auction—in their fucking vile sex-trafficking rituals.

"That's an amazing spin on some really sick shit, Lucian," I retort. "But what about this? What if I say *fuck you, I'm not coming*?"

Lucian purses his lips. "Unfortunately, Calloway, that's not an option. It's just not. And I want to be careful here to explain without emotion, because truly, my boy, I'd absolutely hate it to end this way. But if you don't come, your death would not be a threat, but a fact. As would your brothers' deaths. And, quite unfortunately, their mates as well."

Kane and Rook feel like loaded missiles behind my back. It's all I can do to keep them at bay with a commanding, wide-palmed hand. They don't normally take orders from their younger brother, but in this case, they do me the favor.

Fuck me. The tables have certainly turned.

I glance back at my brothers and then at Kylie and Blair. And then, I set my gaze on Lucian.

"The choice is yours," he says, an infuriating smirk cresting his mouth. "But the consequences are completely in my control."

At his words, a deep groan escapes Rook's throat, and when I look over my shoulder, I can tell he's hanging by a thread as whatever fucking pain-voodoo powers Lucian has start to consume his body. My eldest brother is a big fucking bastard, and his pain tolerance is unlike anything I've ever seen, but he's no match for Lucian.

Rook only stays on his feet for ten seconds before he's on his knees with a clenched jaw and his beloved Kylie trying to help him with concern.

"Stop!" I demand. "Just fucking stop."

"And why would I stop?" Lucian questions. "Because you've had an epiphany that attending the selection process is not only a wonderful opportunity for you, but something you are happily going to do?"

When I don't answer right away, I hear Kane fall to his knees from behind me on a strangled groan.

"No, no, no!" Blair screams. "Kane!"

And when I look over my shoulder, the pain in my brothers' eyes and the terror on their fated mates' faces is too fucking much.

"Fine!" I shout. "You can stop with the bullshit! I'll come!"

Lucian lets out a hearty laugh, and with a little twist of his wrist, he stops my brothers' pain.

"But just me," I add through a tight jaw. "Kane and Rook and their mates aren't necessary."

"Nonsense. This is a family affair," Lucian declares with a

clap. "It'll be all or none," he says and purposefully steps closer to Kylie…and then a moment later does the same to Blair. "And I know the three of you are smart enough to understand the implications of each."

Oh yeah, motherfucker. The implications are downright impossible to miss.

He looks at the women again, and both of my brothers are strung tight as fucking bows. It's clear Lucian Wrath is willing to do anything to get what he wants, and unfortunately for us, he outmatches us in the worst kind of way.

"So…what shall it be?" he questions and walks over toward Kylie to just barely touch the ends of her brown hair. "Everyone… or no one?"

I scrub a hand down my face, desperate to figure a way out of this mess, but there is no way out. Our hands are fucking tied. Our body count stacked too high. All our transgressions against the elite point straight to a death sentence.

I don't trust Lucian, but I don't doubt he's a man of his word when it comes to consequences, I think in my mind, hoping to hell Rook can use his telepathy to tap into me.

I have no idea if Lucian is a shield, but I'd prefer to have this conversation without scaring Kylie and Blair even more than they already are.

I want to murder this fucking fuck, Rook pushes into my head.

Yeah, well, clearly, we're out-fucking-matched, I think.

Kane says his offer isn't saying death…at least…not yet, Rook pushes into my head.

Kane's not wrong. Going along with Lucian might be the only chance we have to survive, I answer back. *We gotta do this, man. I fucking hate it, but it's all we've got right now.*

"Looks like the Slaters are headed to New York," Rook growls.

"Beautiful." Lucian smiles. "If I may make a suggestion?"

We all just stare at him.

"Pack your finest. We have many exciting events to attend."

3

ROMY

UTTER-YELLOW SILK SKIMS MY LEGS AS I WALK into the massive ballroom of the mansion set somewhere outside of New York City, a glass of wine in hand and a sour feeling in my stomach that's kept me from eating all day.

This morning, after I found four new gowns my mother approved of in Neiman Marcus and stopped home to pack them safely in a garment bag, my father drove me to the airport and escorted me all the way to the gate—somehow—to make sure I got on the plane.

We didn't speak much, but truly, we didn't need to. His decision to send me off to be sold and my sense of betrayal as a result are like two ends of the same wooden board—connected forever, but in no way will they ever meet in the middle without chopping everything up into a million tiny pieces.

Trust me, we've already argued; there's no changing this.

Upon arrival at Newark, New Jersey's airport, I was escorted right off the plane into a waiting Porsche on the tarmac by two men in black suits and put in the back seat without so much as a *hey, how ya doing?*

The windows were tinted in both directions, making it nearly impossible to see outside as we drove at an incredibly fast speed out of the airport and up into some suburb of New York I'm imagining to be Westchester.

The truth, though, is that besides the luscious green grounds and intimidating gray stone of the biggest mansion I've ever seen, I haven't a clue about where they've brought me.

Where they've brought all of us.

Women of a distinct age group—*mine*—mingle and mill about the large space, drinking fancy cocktails and whispering to one another in excited flutters of curiosity and intrigue. There are no men in the room as of yet, other than the gruff-looking security guards at the doors, which is at least a small comfort, but the energy feels off, nonetheless.

Despite a wide array of colorful gowns and ethnicities, the group of women still manages to feel similar. The perfectly crafted makeup, the attempt at wealth on an array of budgets—the sexual nature of their appearance in every way.

We're products here, not people. And our families sent us *willingly.*

My breath comes out in a shaky huff as I set down my now-empty glass on a passing tray and force myself to move deeper into the room. I don't want to participate, but I do want to blend in, and loitering at the door in abject horror is exactly the opposite of what everyone else seems to be doing.

I reach for my phone in my purse to find distraction and only remember that they took it, along with my luggage, when I arrived at the airport and *conveniently forgot* to give it back, when I come up empty-handed.

My bags were in my room before I was, but my phone is long gone. *Probably at the bottom of a bucket of blood or whatever the fuck vampires get a kick out of.*

I have a feeling that's by design, not coincidence.

"Hi," I'm surprised to hear from my left, spinning me around in a whirl. The young blond woman smiles and shrugs. "I'm Abigail. What's your name?"

"Romy," I answer, trying not to take the level of unease I'm feeling about becoming a vampire's plaything out on her and succeeding partially. I'm not sure what my face is doing, but if she asks, I'll blame it on RBF.

"Romy," she repeats kindly. "I like that a lot."

"Thanks." I clear my throat. "Sorry. I'm not trying to be… I'm just nervous."

"Really?" she asks, surprised. "I've been waiting for this for, like, forever. My mom started talking about the Selection when I was a kid. She says it's the highest honor and philanthropic in ways the public would never be able to understand. You and I, and all these women…we're the *reason* these vampires will continue to exist. You don't think that's exhilarating?"

I snort. "Yeah, not really. I mean, don't get me wrong, my mom has always told me the same thing. I just…"

"Don't believe her?"

I shake my head. "Think it's *rosied up* a little bit too much. You're not worried about not having a say in who picks you?"

She balks for just a fraction of a moment before smiling again. "No. I have no reason to be. These are all the literal strongest, most powerful, richest, handsomest men in the world. Any of them would be better than the crop of human men out there."

When I grimace, she laughs.

"Oh, come on. You really think these vampires are sending three a.m. *you up?* messages in between unsolicited dick pics? Because that's what I'm getting outside of here, and I know just from looking at you, you are too."

"Okay, I'll give you that it's not great out there. But surely there are good ones. Romantics. Men who would never participate in something like…*this.*"

She reaches out to squeeze my hand, a motion intended to comfort me. It's funny, though, because her naïveté about what's really happening here doesn't console me at all. "It's going to be amazing, Romy. You'll see. And if you need someone to hang out with until you're convinced and vent out all your worries, you can hang with me." She looks around the room conspiratorially before lowering her voice to a whisper. "Some of these other ladies seem a little uptight."

For the first time since entering this ballroom of doom, I laugh. It's not as if I feel good about any of this yet, but maybe it's not such a bad idea to have a pseudo-friend to stick with through it.

I nod. "Okay, yeah. Thanks. That's really nice of you."

"Come on," Abigail says, grabbing me by the hand. "Let's go get another cocktail and a bite of something to eat. Shall we?"

"We shall."

It's not like I have many other options right now anyway.

4

CAL

LUCIAN DIDN'T WASTE ANY TIME MAKING MY brothers and me follow through.

And now, here I stand, inside a luxury mansion, surrounded by elite vampires listening to my uncle address the room.

"Welcome, gentlemen, to Viewing Night," Lucian announces. "For the next two hours, you're invited to observe and learn about the pool of exceptional women we've gathered for this year's Selection. I know many of you are new to the process, and we'll be walking you through it as necessary, but the Council's biggest piece of advice is to enjoy it. You'll only have your first Selection once, and I must say…there's nothing quite like that thrill."

My jaw locks tightly as I lean against the wall in the back of the room, trapped in the hell of watching my uncle and his elder peers talk about this event like it's some sort of fucking trip to an amusement park.

I'm wearing a tux and holding a glass of bourbon in my hand, but the liquor is untouched and the setting is the least deserving of formal wear I've ever seen.

It's fucking disgusting, plain and simple. And if I had any other option at all, I wouldn't be anywhere near it.

As things stand, though, I'm stuck here. Kane and Blair and Rook and Kylie have been confined somewhere out of sight since we arrived, and I've been tucked under *Uncle* Lucian's wing.

And because of the tremendous exhibition of power he made during our first meeting, I haven't gone rogue. Hell, he might be one of the most powerful vampire I've ever met. There's no telling what he'd do to Rook, Kane, and their mates before I even had a chance to find them.

I'm trapped—both physically and emotionally—for the time being.

"Calloway," my uncle calls from the front of the room, startling both me and the large group of men around me. I expected to be the unspoken elephant in the room for a bit—to be cast as an outsider as a further form of punishment.

Several sets of angry eyes find mine in a sneer, and the ones who don't are openly curious. A hundred vampires, all waiting for me to make a wrong move. As the quietest brother of the Slater trio, I've never been under this much scrutiny in my life.

But I guess that's the point.

"Yes?" Even the simple word feels like a bitter betrayal of my tongue. To be here. To be compliant. Everything about this is an assault on all that I stand for.

"Come up here, please."

My jaw locks around a nasty lack of choice. He's taken away my autonomy completely by separating me from my brothers, and he knows it. But he'll be the only fool if he thinks my compliance is built to last. I *will* be ruining him and this place and all these men when the time is right.

I vow it.

Weaving through the agitated group of wealthy pricks, I make my way to the front, only stopping when my uncle sets a hand atop my shoulder and spins me to face the room. My body is stiff, and my eyes scan the space for threats.

"Gentlemen, I know some of you are wondering about the presence of Calloway here, as most of you know him as a member of our blue-collar class," my uncle announces. "I understand the confusion, but I want you to set aside your preconceived notions about who he is or where he comes from and treat him as one of your own." He chuckles. "Calloway is *my* nephew."

There are a few subtle inhales at the unexpected news, and a quiet murmur of hushed and hurried whispers follows swiftly. Naturally, my ears don't disappoint. I can hear every fucked-up thing they say about my blue-collar background and orphaned childhood, but I shut it out as quickly as it starts.

Opinions of assholes like these are irrelevant, and letting their nonsense clutter my mind will unnecessarily dull my senses.

"He's one of us, of the fourth, previously thought to be extinct, noble bloodline," Lucian continues, shaking my body with a tight squeeze of his still-present hand. "And as such, is a key piece of the Council's long-standing goal for racial purity. If we're to be the best, we need the best. And Calloway...is the *best*. Understand?"

There's a low murmur of understanding and begrudged agreement, but for my part, I'm reeling over the news.

Not only are my brothers and I elite, but our mother was of the *fourth* bloodline that went extinct decades ago? I'm shocked.

But I'm also fucking over this ostentatious display.

Without waiting for permission, I step out from my uncle's hold and back into the crowd, carving my way to the back of the room.

A couple of men laugh, and my uncle joins in—relishing the cute little display of obstinance from their pawn—and then continues with his speech.

"We'll be moving now to the observation room on the second floor. Don't worry about your drinks—there's a bar up there—just follow us swiftly, if you would, to prevent any commingling with the women in the hallway."

As the men file out into the hall, chuckling and festering in evil rapture, a small group of men congregates at my uncle, who is, once again, flagging me over.

Frustrated, I down the glass of bourbon before setting it aside and stride toward them, anger clinging to me like a sturdy companion. It's as though Rook cloaked me in his personality for good measure. He's always been a grumpy-as-fuck bastard.

"Calloway, before we adjourn to the viewing room, I just wanted you to meet *my* brothers," Lucian declares, effectively drawing my eyes to the three men beside him in a snap.

His brothers, meaning one of these men is *my* father.

It's the second time he's caught me off guard in the last five minutes, and by the smile on his face, he's reveling in it.

Regardless, I log information about our sperm donors as both a matter of confirmation and information. The more I know about the men who decided not to raise us, the more ruthless I'll be able to be when I destroy them.

Tall, intimidating, and sickeningly unbothered, my father is immediately recognizable. But of course he is—I, unfortunately, am his spitting image. From our hair to our posture, to the slightly outward camber of our feet, we are of the same blueprint.

He greets me with a jerk of his chin and zero relational warmth, and I return the favor with a look of disgust. The inside, evidently, is where the similarities run dry.

And then he *laughs*. "I don't know, Lucian. I know you said he's mine, but I don't really see the resemblance," he mocks, actively ignoring my matching brown hair, blue eyes, and sharp jaw for a chance at a low blow. "Looks like any other poor fuck playing dress-up in fancy clothes to me."

"Please, Cassian, practice some decorum, I beg of you," Lucian chastises, though his anger falls well short of his eyes. "This isn't the setting for uncivilized behavior."

Good news? I now know my father's name is Cassian. Bad news? He's a fucking piece of shit.

Cassian just keeps laughing, and the two other men—one blond and one dark-haired—laugh right along with him. They don't hesitate to look in my direction the entire time. They want me to feel uncomfortable. They want me to know they think I'm the butt of the joke.

And when the blond and dark-haired men's faces turn up in all-too-familiar smiles, the unbearable news of Rook's and Kane's fathers—and their also shitty personalities—confirms itself too.

Wherever my brothers are, I hope to fuck they're not being subjected to this kind of mental warfare.

"A spade has no problem being called a spade," I eventually say, shrugging an unbothered shoulder. "Which is why I'm sure you don't blink when people call you a prick."

My uncle, the crazy asshole, laughs like he's somehow proud of the reply, heading off my father's angry steam before it can escalate. "Good. Now we're even on the jabs, and we can move on."

The other three, however, take much more offense. They were hoping to crawl under my skin and root there—but it's hard to bully someone who doesn't give a shit.

I only care about the opinions of people I would trade places with—and I wouldn't trade places with these fuckers for a hundred billion dollars.

"I wanted all of you to meet so we could act as a welcoming committee of sorts," Lucian goes on to explain. "If Calloway is going to assimilate among us, he needs to have some stewards." He points toward the dark-haired asshole. "This is Nathanial." And then he points to the blond-headed fuck. "And Ronan."

Neither man offers a smile or their hand.

"Good luck, kid," Cassian—*my fucking father*—spits. He eyes me over his glass of bourbon before snorting in disgust and downing his drink. "You're certainly going to need it." He turns hard blue eyes to Lucian, spilling his evil out for the world to see with no filter. "If I'm his steward, he's dead. How about that?"

Lucian sighs as Cassian walks away, and Rook's and Kane's fathers snicker among themselves.

"Nathanial? Ronan?" Lucian eyes them pointedly. "You owe me this."

"Fine, Luc." Nathanial nods, his mouth set in a firm line, and it's almost uncanny how much Rook looks like his father. "But don't expect me to do it nicely." He shoves into my shoulder as he walks away, and Ronan is the only brother left to consider me.

He shakes the ice in his glass and runs his tongue across his teeth. "My boy look as much like me as you look like Cassian?"

Kane might as well be his fucking mini-me, but I shake my head. "Nope," I lie. "Not even a little bit."

Without so much as another word, Ronan leaves the room to head for the observation space, and my jaw works itself over with the effort not to break in two.

It's one thing to meet your father. It's a whole other thing to come face-to-face with a man who sells and tortures innocent women for sport, knows you're his son…and thinks you're better off dead.

"Come on, Calloway. Let's get moving," Lucian encourages, moving on from the fucked-up family reunion as though it never even happened. "You've got a room of women to see."

I don't say anything—because I can't.

Nothing, *and I mean nothing,* short of burning this whole place to the motherfucking ground will do.

I walk on wooden legs as my uncle escorts me out the door, past a couple of security guys, down a long hallway, and up a grand set of red-carpeted steps. At the top, we make a left and enter a pair of double mahogany doors into a ballroom with a wall of floor-to-ceiling windows along the entire left side.

Male vampires of all ages stand at the glass like a bunch of zoo-goers at the gorilla exhibit, talking among themselves and pointing to various parts of the room below.

The moment I step inside, something stirs in my gut—an instinct that pulls my attention toward the glass with them.

It's unsettling as hell.

And it doesn't matter what the women down there look like; they're all innocent pawns in a rich vampire game.

"It's a one-way mirror," my uncle updates as he guides me toward the viewing glass. "The women down below can't see us. This is an important part of the selection process that allows us the opportunity to see them acting naturally. As I'm sure you could guess, a lot of them have preconceived notions about how they need to be—what look they need to present—and, when they're among us, turn into something of a different personality entirely."

Overwhelming discomfort pricks at each and every one of my senses as we step up to the massive viewing window and peer down into the room full of extravagantly dressed women.

They talk among themselves and laugh and drink, upturning their faces toward us just enough that my stomach flips over.

"If they can't see, why are they looking up here?" I ask, hating myself but needing the information if I'm even going to have a shot in hell at dismantling this place from the inside out.

Lucian smiles. "Keen observation, Calloway."

I don't accept the compliment, but he doesn't care. He takes the inquisition as a personal victory, leaning in even more closely and lowering his voice as he explains.

"For their part, there's a montage of previously bonded couples playing via a projector on the wall above them," he answers. "It's comforting for them to see the happiness on the faces of their predecessors and ancestors, and for our part, it gives us a chance to see their faces more clearly."

Forcing myself to scan the faces of the innocent women below, I log them into my memory and vow internally to set them free from the chains of a fate they cannot and should not have to foresee.

What these men here intend to do with them is both self-serving and morally compromised in every way it can be.

I know there may be a couple among this group of vampires who don't fully understand the implications of buying a woman to use for their own consumption and enrichment of power—or, I don't know, maybe I'm just hoping there are for the sake of my sanity—but the practice is archaic and repulsive, and I can't, in good conscience or moral heart, allow it to go on for another year.

This one will be the end. This one will—

Everything inside me freezes as a face peeks through the crowd below, upturned in something much, much different than a smile.

Her pale-yellow dress further highlights the sick pallor of her skin as she watches the supposed movie rolodex of couples who came before her, and a grimace turns down the corners of her perfectly pink mouth.

She looks…wrong here.

My body leans toward the glass before I even realize I've moved, and a strange pressure spreads through my chest, tightening with every second my eyes stay locked on her.

It's on the tip of my tongue to ask her name, but the thought slams to a halt as something hits me with the force of a fist to the gut.

The room fades.

The noise disappears.

All that exists is *her*.

And the terrifying certainty blooming inside my chest.

This is it, I think, as wonder and regret and something dangerously close to grief twist at every nerve-ending inside my body. *This is the feeling my brothers both had. This is the change. Immediate. All-consuming.* Irreversible.

She—*whoever she is*—is my fated mate.

I know it as well as I know that Calloway Slater is my own name.

Suddenly, the pull to the glass makes perfect sense.

But it also means everything about this situation just got a hell of a lot more complicated.

5

ROMY

HIS IS OFFICIALLY THE NIGHT THAT WILL NEVER end.

Look, I know vampires don't need sleep—or food or water, for that matter—but I, for one, could use a bed… or possibly a coma I won't wake up from. Honestly, I'm not picky.

Abigail drags me over by the elbow to yet another group of women, officially making me the adopted puppy she can't get rid of without a turn of conscience now.

I pick another flute of champagne off a passing tray, willing myself to sip it with intention rather than downing the damn thing—like I did with the two before it—because my head is starting to feel a wee bit tipsy.

I'm not much of a drinker, and my stomach is still empty, so the staggering effects of alcohol are well on their way to opening me up to even more vulnerability.

At the same time, the idea of numbing myself as a way to cope with the batshit-crazy enthusiasm of the gross majority of these women is compelling, to say the least.

"Romy, this is Chastity, Margo, and Hillary," Abigail says by way of introduction. "Romy, these are the girls." They all giggle at Abigail's mayoral ability to somehow already know nearly everyone in the room after an hour of mingling, and I suck in a breath before slapping on a smile and offering a halfhearted wave.

"Hi," I say. "Nice to meet all of you."

"I like your dress, Romy," the woman I think Abigail said was Hillary adds. Her smile seems genuine, if a little timid, and I latch on to the authenticity immediately.

"Thanks. My mother didn't love the yellow, but I convinced her because of the fabric. The only thing I've been wishing all night is that I could have talked her into a blazer. It's freezing in here."

"I know!" Hillary agrees, officially breaking us off into our own little conversation as Abigail and the other two cackle about something else and point to the big projection screens at the top of the wall.

"What is that that they're playing up there?" I ask Hillary, hoping she can break it down without sounding like it's an opportunity to win a million-dollar lottery. Abigail's been great—really. I've been included and the time has passed exponentially faster than it would have if I'd been left to fester in my own thoughts, but the delight she holds in every fiber of her being over this whole charade is starting to wear on me.

"Oh. I think one of the other girls said it's a slideshow from some of the past bonding nights or something. I guess it's supposed to get us excited about meeting our own vampire." Her voice doesn't hold quite as much disdain as my own, but it's not euphoric either.

I count the change of pace as a win.

"Is it working for you like it's working for me?" I ask sarcastically, and she laughs. *Thank God.*

"It is what it is. I just…hope he's nice. And hot. A six-pack and an unbelievably white smile wouldn't hurt, you know?"

"Oh yeah. I mean, I could go for men who wouldn't—"

Before I can reply fully, I'm hit with a sudden wave of discomfort. My stomach turns and jumps, sending a jolt of panic into my throat I can't swallow down. It's the weirdest feeling of *awareness* I've ever had, and for lack of a better explanation, it feels like someone's *watching* me—closely.

Spinning in a tight but slow circle, I scan the women around me for a lingering stare, but I come up empty entirely. They're all occupied, either chatting with one another or watching the sideshow slideshow above, and the security, too, seems to be conveniently missing.

It must be the alcohol taking a turn for the worse.

"Hey, are you okay?" Hillary asks. Not only did I stop talking to exercise a bout of paranoia right in the middle of a sentence, but I'm holding my stomach like I'm about to be hit with the shits. I can't imagine how it looks, but truly, I feel too bad to care.

Increasingly worried that I'll get sick right here in the middle of this reception, I excuse myself with a polite *be right back* to Hillary and take off at a speed walk for the main door.

The coast looks clear as I push through the heavy wood, intent on finding a bathroom and pronto, but just like this whole farce, it's nothing more than an illusion.

A Hulk-sized security dude in a black suit steps in front of me and holds up a hand as the other goons come toward me from the opposite end of the hall. They're pushing racks of some kind of clothing, I think, and the wheels at the bottom all rolling together create an overbearing hum on the plushness of the carpet.

"I just need to go to the bath—"

"One moment," the man with his hand still held out in front of me interrupts.

As the racks roll by me and through the doors I've just come out of, I get a better look at their contents, and my own—stomach contents, specifically—take a turn for the worse.

Holy shit. Those are racks of lingerie!

Panties. Corsets. Bras. Teddies. The whole nine fucking yards. It's a mobile Victoria's Secret in this place, and I am *horrified* at the possibilities of what that means.

If I weren't already feeling sick, I'd be charging toward it now.

"Please," I beg. "I really need to go to the restroom. I feel like I'm going to be sick."

Eyes widening in terror, he says something curt into a microphone attached to his chest and waves me forward, and I follow him in a hurry to a door at the end of the hall. It's just a swing door—no lock or anything that would make me feel even remotely good about going into a supposed bathroom—but I don't hesitate for fear that he'll rescind the offer.

Moving quickly, I take the trash can from the corner and prop it in front of the entrance when it closes behind me just for some modicum of comfort. I know in reality that the strength of a trash can is nothing against the strength of a vampire—or worse, many vampires. If they want in here with me, they're coming.

Still. *Maybe they won't come in if they hear me cry.*

Gripping the vanity with mottled hands, I do the kind of deep breathing I learned in Pilates.

Long-count inhales, hard, audible exhales. It's like I'm in labor and Lamaze-ing it up.

But I'm so fucking overwhelmed it's not even funny. To not want to be here in the first place was enough. But to be slapped with the reality of those racks of *nothingness* they're trying to pass off as clothes is worthy of all-out panic.

My heart pounds and my ears whoosh as I work to find some semblance of calm in the chaos.

Okay. Okay. It's okay. I don't know how it's okay, but it's going. To. Be. Okay.

It has to be.

Breathing in through my nostrils and out through my mouth, I take gulps of air and do my best to hold on to the nourishment of oxygen as they move through me.

I consider myself in the mirror—my makeup and curled hair and too-low-cut dress—and try to filter through the emotions that got me here.

Disgust. *Obviously.*

But more than that, it was intuition.

An overbearing feeling that sent me running for this bathroom for a moment of clarity and the, possibly naïve, hope that I could find some level of comfort in what's happening.

I don't know why I thought any of those things or why the gut instinct persists now, but when the ogre outside the bathroom bangs a comically gentle fist on the door, I move my ass. First to the toilet to empty my bladder and give my stomach the chance to settle, and then to the sink to both wash my hands and splash a minuscule amount of cold water on the back of my neck.

Moving the trash can carefully back into place, I pull open the door and step outside to find the man blissfully gone. He's down the hall now, wrestling a final rack of lingerie with another dude, and it takes everything inside me not to take off in the opposite direction of the big, fancy, and now risqué-bra-and-panty-filled ballroom at a dead run.

Short-term, it sounds amazing.

Surely there'd be a door to the outside and a patch of woods I could navigate to a road where I can hitchhike.

But I'm too smart to pigeonhole myself into a scary movie outcome where the woman blindly runs right at danger while the whole audience is chanting for her to stop. *These are vampires, Romy. Compared to theirs, your run is the equivalent of a legless crawl.*

With one last huff, I adjust my dress and take a step back toward the ballroom. But a door across the hallway opens and pulls me up short.

It's a man—dressed in formal attire and a far sight more important-looking than the ogres working security—and the door swinging closed behind him is the male bathroom mirror of my own.

Adjusting his jacket and buttoning it with one hand, he looks up from the carpet and straight into my eyes, and I'm transported to a simpler time in the blink of an eye.

To playgrounds and colored pencils and plaid-skirt uniforms. To fantasies of noble princes and castles in the country and a fairy tale of my own.

I'm not in Dracula's scary lair anymore—I'm back in my adolescent days at the Boston Preparatory Academy in Massachusetts.

To the days when I was a little girl with a big crush on an older boy, and the stars in her eyes to prove it.

He's all grown up now, but he's the same boy I fawned over back then. I'd bet on it.

"Cal?" I ask, my whole being incredulous beyond belief. "Calloway Slater? Is that you?"

His eyes snap up into a scrutinous scan of my face and then body, widening noticeably as he takes me in. It's the weirdest feeling—it's as if he saw me before, but seeing me now that I've said his name, he's seeing me for the first time all over again.

"No fucking way," he murmurs in answer, which, completely despite myself, makes me laugh and nod at the same time.

"Yep."

"Romy Spencer?" he asks then, seemingly still needing the confirmation.

"That's me," I reply dumbly, raising my hands out to the sides. As the nostalgia wears off, the reality of seeing the boy I once fantasized about all grown up and *here*, of all places, sends me to the pits of despair. "What…what are you doing here?"

His jaw is tight, and his voice is painfully quiet. "You know why."

He's here…with the other male vampires…to select…

I swallow hard, taking an involuntary step back.

He notices, but I'm not surprised. Calloway Slater always noticed everything.

6

CAL

ROMY SPENCER IS THE WOMAN IN THE YELLOW dress.

Romy Spencer is my *fated mate.*

The three-years-younger-than-me adorable girl who used to chase me around the playground begging to hang out with me instead of the mean-girl clique her teacher wanted her to be a part of. The girl who treated me and my brothers as her equals in a sea of people who looked down on us. The girl whom I often wondered about when we left our first foster family and were moved out of Boston Prep and into the public school across town.

It's the worst news of my life to finally come face-to-face with her here. *And it's the most anything has ever made sense to find out she's the one the universe picked for me.*

Everything in me locks on her, like there's no world where she isn't mine.

And even though it's been years since I've seen her, I feel as if I know her more than I know myself. As if my entire being is attuned to everything that is her.

Every breath she takes feels like it echoes through me and her visible fear hits me like a blade to the ribs.

Right now, she's scared of me. I can see it in the light blue of her eyes and the slight shake of her legs.

I don't blame her—seeing me like this, here, can only paint one picture about the kind of man I've grown into.

"I'm sorry to see you here," I say quietly, rubbing the back of my neck and begging the burn inside me to gentle. I don't want to frighten her any more than I already have—intrinsically, it kills me to scare her at all. "But I *am* glad to see you."

Because even now—even like this—being near her feels like finding something I didn't know I'd been missing my entire life.

"You're a…"

Vampire.

I nod, leaving the word silent between us. It's not even a question what she's thinking. I can read it as though it's my own thought. There may be a few adjectives in front of it—*evil, greedy, sadistic, morally bankrupt*—but the noun is the same. I am a vampire. And by being here, I am the scariest version of one.

One who takes. One who lies. One who thinks he's above everyone and everything.

I can't remember a moment when I've longed for simpler times of childhood, but right now, I do. I long for a time in the past when Romy Spencer and I were attached at the hip and things like humans and vampires and bloodlines and class systems were never discussed.

A time when innocence was at the foundation of everything.

Everything inside me wants to throw her over my shoulder and run her straight out of this fucking nightmare. Truthfully, my body is strongly championing for it and I have to clench my hands into fists just to keep my composure.

Now isn't the time to fuck up. Not only would I be risking my brothers' and their mates' lives, I'd be risking hers too. And fuck me, I wouldn't be able to handle that.

Romy might be clueless about what she means to me—that she's managed to become the equivalent of my entire world in what feels like a nanosecond and an eternity at the same time—but every cell inside my body is *aware*.

"But…I didn't… Cal…" She pauses, her voice shaking as it breaks.

She knows exactly why I'm here and the monster it makes me, even if it confuses the memories she has of me as a kid. She *knows*. I can feel it in the tremble of her hands and the way her heart races and her breaths come out stilted. And I see it written all over her face.

Unlike most of the women gathered in that ballroom, Romy *knows* the life beyond the veil—understands that the future they've painted isn't exactly drawn to scale.

I don't know how or why she knows—or if the fear she carries was instilled by her parents or born of natural instincts—but I hope with every fiber of my being she'll carry it as close to the vest as possible until I figure out how to get us both out of this.

Until I figure out how to end the auction altogether.

"Hey!" one of the gofers responsible for security shouts, noticing us standing together for the first time.

They don't want the men and women mingling yet, for fear that it'll place some sort of doubt in a woman's mind about the man who picks her. That she'll fret over not being picked by someone else. That it'll expose this whole mess for what it is and cause a rebellion.

The Council may be in control of this situation, but what they are not is invincible.

They need volunteers. They need participation. Maybe not as a whole, but at least in part, because to take an entire group of women by force would be remarkably harder.

Maybe, just maybe, there's something to that I can use.

When Romy and I don't move immediately, the security guard stalks toward us, his mouth moving as he, no doubt, makes a report to someone in a higher position. The last thing I want to do is call more attention to Romy—and make no mistake, there is already extra attention on me—so even though it kills me, I clear my throat to prepare myself and then send her away.

I haven't had the chance to explain. Or to find some way to convince her I'm here as a mercenary behind enemy lines. Or that the boy she knew is still inside me.

She fears me still, but there's no time to make it right.

"You'd better get back in there."

I want to say more—to put her at ease *somehow*. But I know nothing I could say in the span of two seconds would help.

To promise to see her again would be a threat.

To offer conspiratorial unease with no explanation would only build her own.

Turning swiftly, I make my way to the stairs as she heads for the ballroom, and I don't turn around to double-check. The jolting shock of distance away from her—from my fated mate—makes me feels almost as painful as when Lucian's power of agony took me to my fucking knees.

But my ears never leave her. I can hear her exchange with the guard, and every single part of it puts my teeth on edge.

"Get back inside, please. There's to be no mingling with the men without permission."

"I was just saying hello to an old friend whom I was surprised to see. I'm sorry."

Fuck. An old friend. I can't blame her for sharing a secret she didn't know to keep, but it's unfortunate, nonetheless. I have no doubts I'll need to be even more alert now—that my uncle and God knows who else from the Council will be watching the two of us interact even more closely.

If I'm not careful, she'll quickly become their next target for my weakness.

My uncle's eyes find my face as soon as I enter the ballroom and head for the bar. While the bartender pours my bourbon, I scan the rest of the room to test the level of both interest and distrust.

Nathanial, Cassian, and Ronan—the other three Wrath brothers—stand at the glass like the rest of the older elites, far too absorbed in their own appraisal of the women below to notice anything else happening in the room.

Most of the men their age are the same.

Which isn't exactly surprising. Any vampire who finds himself back here at their advanced age—needing to purchase another woman after whatever he did to the last one—clearly isn't known for restraint or conscience.

The thought alone leaves a bitter taste in my mouth.

The younger elites are a different story. Many of them watch me openly, their eyes flicking over my suit, my posture, my background—judging every inch of my presence here without even attempting to hide it.

If I open my mind to the noise of it, I can hear the assumptions forming in real time. Speculation about why my uncle brought me here. What role I'm meant to play.

But the most surprising part of it all? None of them actually seems to know.

Assumptions they've made? Aplenty. *But real information?* That's largely lacking among the entire crowd.

And that makes me even more interested in my uncle, his motives, and what the hell my brothers and I have managed to get ourselves involved in.

I have a really bad feeling that we've just barely scraped the surface.

7

ROMY

Y WHOLE BODY TREMBLES AS I'M USHERED back into the ballroom by security, and the door closes behind me in such a dominant way it's clear that even if I tried to fight him, he'd force me inside here.

I'm overwhelmed, to say the least, so much so that my brain doesn't even know where to start.

The sight of Calloway Slater…*here*—at a vampire auction designed to bid on women like me, so they can have the best selection of human blood possible.

The reaction of security when they saw me talking to Cal outside the bathrooms and how it wasn't allowed.

The feeling of someone watching me so intently it burns.

The presence of a whole big-ass group of men, like Cal but potentially worse, somewhere in this palatial mansion that we don't know about.

And last but not freaking least, the *lingerie*.

The racks and racks of lingerie that now stare back at me from across the room.

I lick my lips and swallow hard as I rejoin the group of women, the majority of whom have fallen like vultures onto the rolling racks to pick out their negligees with excitement.

There's even a little bit of bitching and arguing over the most-wanted pieces, and my stomach turns over on itself at the sound of it.

Abigail is deep in the thick of it, so I linger in the back, hoping to spot another familiar face or see at least a flicker of someone else who doesn't think this is the greatest day of her life. I know I'm right to be on edge, but with the way everyone else isn't, I feel a little insane.

Thankfully, Hillary finds me before I can find her, and while it's only a small balm on an oozing, festering wound of anxiety, it's at least something.

"Hey, you okay?" she asks.

I don't know how it's possible, but it feels like I shake my head and nod at the same time, the flurry of a feeling I've never, ever had before invading my entire body. It's need and unease and an overwhelming sense of incompleteness. "Yeah. I'm…yeah. I'm fine."

Poor Hillary would only be confused, even if I tried to name the real emotions running through me right now, so I settle for being vague. It doesn't help her understand either, but she must be a good person because she smiles anyway.

"You missed the spiel while you were in the bathroom," she updates. "They said these are our *bonding night* outfits, hand-selected by the men themselves for us to pick from. That got a lot of the girls wondering if whichever one they pick will have something to do with who bids on them. Like a kismet sort of thing?"

She shrugs and then links her hands together, picking at the cuticle of one thumb with the other.

"How come you're not choosing yours?" I ask, using her nervous behavior to ground my own.

She hesitates for a brief moment but then lowers her voice to a whisper. "I don't know. I guess I will at some point. It just… seems a little weird."

Thank God. Someone with normal thoughts!

"Okay, right? It is weird. It's…it's *crazy!*" Her chin jerks back at my zeal, so I clear my throat and try to dial it back. "Sorry. I just… I'm overwhelmed. I don't really understand the thrill of the whole thing in the first place, and…" I lower my voice to a soft whisper. Hillary reads my intention and moves closer. "Out there…when I went to the bathroom. I…ran into one of the vampires. And he's someone I used to know…"

"What?" she asks, her eyes widening exponentially.

I nod. "Back when I was a kid. We…we went to a prep school together for a little less than a year. He's obviously grown now." *So freaking grown it's crazy intimidating. Tall, strong—unbelievably handsome. I swear Calloway Slater is cut from a God-tier cloth.* "But yeah. I…I guess I didn't expect that they'd be men who'd, like, walked among us before. My mom always talked about the elites like they were locked away somewhere in a gilded, exclusive town or something."

"Did he talk to you? What did he say?" Hillary asks, her intensity growing with each word. But as Abigail approaches with a red teddy in hand, I make a conscious choice to shut my trap.

"Sorry. Later," I whisper to Hillary. "But please don't tell anyone."

Something I can't quite explain tells me not to say anything about this to a large group of women. Especially Abigail. She's been nothing but friendly since I arrived, but there's not a person in here she hasn't talked to at least twice. *Who knows what she's sharing around when she does.*

"Hey, guys!" Abigail greets cheerfully, clutching the tiny sheer dress she's just picked out from a rack like it's the best thing she's ever laid eyes on. "Aren't you going to go pick something? The selection is getting thin."

Hillary nods, scurrying toward the rack at the news, and I shrug before following in her footsteps at a much slower pace.

I find a rack that's largely deserted because it only has a few plain black pieces left and start sliding through them slowly. My hand shakes on each hanger as I move them from one side of the rack to the other.

Yikes.

Double yikes.

Ew.

I don't really see anything other than thin lace and black, but I choose one for the simple fact that it offers a full-coverage panty.

Never, in my wildest dreams, did I think choosing something just because it wouldn't show my actual vagina would be the safe option of the bunch, but here we are.

On shaky knees, I rejoin Hillary and Abigail and a group of other women whose names I can't remember, and I tuck the corset and panty set over my arm like a waiter at a fancy restaurant would do with a napkin. It's really the only option since it's a similar amount of fabric, and the more I hold it out and see it, the more I freak out in my mind.

"God, I can't wait for tomorrow night," one of the girls says, practically dancing in place.

"What's tomorrow night?" I ask, kicking myself for avoiding the damn schedule they offered when they first took me to my room.

"It's the co-ed mixer," Abigail explains. "It's the first time we'll be in the room with all the men at once. Didn't you read your schedule?"

Co-ed mixer? I almost want to laugh. Or cry. I don't know. It's all feeling very *The Bachelor* but with a lot fewer roses and a lot more blood.

"I forgot to take one," I lie. Hillary smiles like she knows.

"Oh, I have an extra. I'll grab it out of my room for you when we go back tonight," Abigail offers.

"Thanks."

"No problem." Abigail smiles, and a little giggle escapes her throat. "Honestly, I can't imagine I'd be able to properly pick out any of my outfits without the actual schedule!"

A bell rings over the loudspeaker, startling me entirely and sending the rest of the room into a round of applause. When it quiets slightly, a disembodied, rich, haughty male voice comes over the intercom.

"Ladies, thank you for a delightful opening evening of this year's Selection. We hope you've had a wonderful time convening with women of your equal tonight and cannot wait to meet you ourselves tomorrow. Please dress in similar formal attire and be ready by six fifteen. Security will escort you back to your rooms now. Please, our darlings, rest well. For the rest of the weekend holds more excitement than you can imagine."

The whole group breaks out into a cry of cheers again, tittering and jabbering as we head toward the massive doors in one giant group.

I keep close to Abigail and Hillary as they move us through with a wave of their arms before closing and locking the doors to the ballroom behind us. Red velvet ropes stretch across the grand staircase to the left, as they usher us to the right and down to the other stairs at the end of the hall.

I crane my neck, trying to get a look up and into the roped-off area, knowing that's where Cal went before, but when the rest of the group gets bunched up behind me, security gives me a stern gesture to move my ass.

"What are you looking at?" Hillary whispers, glancing over her shoulder just briefly as I link elbows with her.

"That's where he went," I say vaguely, hoping she'll understand that I'm talking about Cal. "I think they're all up there somewhere."

"You think they're…here? In the house?"

I nod, and her lips suck into her mouth with a healthy mix of fear and curiosity. My mixture leans a little more heavily toward terrified, but compared to the others, who are still gabbing like this is a day camp for wealthy girls, she's practically panicked.

I can tell by the look on her face she'd love nothing more than to come to my room for a little while to talk, but the security ogres make it clear that's not an option. A guard stands by each of our doors, waiting for us to arrive before double-checking the ID bracelets they gave us and letting us inside.

It's solo time, plain and simple. Or, you know, a fancy prison.

Abigail is far too gracious for my liking when she asks her

guard for permission to come back into the hallway to give me a schedule. He nods, reluctantly, and she thanks him like he's doing her a *favor*.

I can't, for the life of me, comprehend how they got all these women so trained to think this is good. To have them thanking the damn security guards for allowing basic human rights!

It's preposterous.

"Here you go," she says, smiling brightly as she hands it over to me.

"Thanks, Abigail."

Hillary glances back from her spot down the hall before going into her room, and I give her a subtle nod to confirm we'll figure out another time to talk.

"Go on," the security guard urges when I guess I linger just a little too long. "To your room, please."

I swallow hard before nodding and complying, walking swiftly down the long, wood-walled, vaulted hall to the very end. My room is the last on the left, and at my door, security is ready and waiting. I pause briefly to scan the two-story ceilings for something nefarious like cameras or hidden doors, but when I come up empty and my guard starts to frown, I step inside.

He pulls a key out of his pocket as he's closing the door, and a wave of panic so strong I can't fight it washes over me. "Um, excuse me? What are you doing? Are you locking me *in*?"

His smile is not at all comforting as he snorts. "Trust me, honey. I'm doing this for your protection."

Without waiting for a reply, he shuts the door in my face and turns the lock with a click, and my throat closes so hard I can barely find the air to breathe.

Locking me in for *my* protection?

No free will whatsoever?

Another party tomorrow night, but this time, add in some vampires?

Ha. Ha-ha-ha.

Dear God. What in the world have my parents gotten me into?

8

CAL

*A*S THE WOMEN LEAVE THE ROOM FOLLOWING the announcement from the president of the Council, I walk away from the mirror and loosen the knot on my tie slightly. The choker is uncomfortable for a blue-collar guy like me on a good day, but here, it feels even more like a noose.

It's a symbol of how trapped Lucian has me, the feeling tightening with every minute that goes by without a plan.

In addition, the energy it's taken to avoid watching Romy for the rest of the evening since returning from the bathroom has damn near depleted me, and no matter how twisted it may sound, I'm relieved to have her and the rest of the women on their way to be locked in their rooms.

A precaution—along with having a gofer security guard outside each and every single door, my uncle explained earlier—that is taken to keep the men from losing control and sullying the women or their blood by claiming it too soon.

Because a sense of propriety and moral conscience here are not enough in a group of wild animals.

There are no words to describe the depravity they flaunt as tradition. There are no words to describe the damage I want to do because of it.

"Gentlemen!" my uncle calls over the din of discussion among the others. "Please, if everyone could convene for just a moment, we'd like to go over some housekeeping business about tomorrow night and the auction itself."

Taking a sip from my bourbon, I linger to the side while the others make their way toward the Council members, who are all lighting cigars and taking celebratory puffs like they've just signed a multimillion-dollar corporate contract or welcomed a baby into the family.

Cassian, Nathanial, and Ronan pull their own cigars from their pockets and light up, having been through the selection process before and obviously knowing it was coming.

I swallow around a knot in my throat and do my best to listen for Romy—to hear anything I can from her room—but come up empty.

The seclusion of the women, I suppose, is a technique born of years of practice as well. Most rebellions find their strength in numbers, and if they're alone, they'll do a hell of a lot less talking. I don't know how many other vampires here have a gift like mine, but I'm not naïve enough to assume I'm unique.

Hopeful, sure. But not stupid.

"Thank you, everyone, for a great opening night," an older man my uncle introduced earlier as the president of the Elite Council announces with a smile. "I hope you'll recognize the amazing talent we've gathered this year and thank the men you've chosen to do your groundwork appropriately."

There are several cheers of recognition and agreement, and Lucian steps forward to take the figurative pulpit from the president.

"Thank you, Narris," Lucian says before looking out toward the crowd. "And thank you, everyone, for being here. As is tradition, it's my job to ready you for what you'll be seeing over the next couple of days and explaining how it works. Tomorrow night, we'll be mingling with the women in the lower ballroom, and you'll get your first chance to learn a little about their personalities, as well as get a closer inspection of the allure of their blood."

Excitement rolls through the men in front of me in a terrifying wave, and it's all I can do to keep my fist from shattering my glass.

"Yes, I know." Lucian chuckles. "It's very exciting, and the temptation will be high. But that's why I must caution you that at this stage of the process, physical contact with the women is strictly forbidden. No touching. No kissing. And absolutely no tasting. The sanctity of their purity and our obligation to a smooth bonding night process requires this control from you. I trust I have all your good word that you'll uphold this rule?"

"Yes."

"Yes!"

"Of course."

"Unfortunately, yes."

"Yes," I agree to a chorus of similar responses throughout

the room. It kills me to justify the edict with a response, but my uncle, I can tell, is listening specifically for my voice.

"Good. Brilliant. Now, let's move on to the details of the auction, shall we?" Lucian claps and smiles. "Two nights from now, we'll convene in the viewing room in the east wing. Your assigned seat will be labeled, and with it, you'll find an iPad. This is the device you'll use to enhance your viewing of the women and where you'll place your silent bid. Each woman will be numbered randomly, and they'll be presented in lots of ten, to keep the confusion and time to make a decision to a minimum."

Lots of ten. Like fucking cattle. I fight the urge to grimace.

But Lucian just keeps prattling on. "There are no secondary bids, so please, I beg of you, make your selection carefully and put your very best offer forward. If you're outbid on your choice, you'll be moved to the secondary selection lot with the remaining women, and the process will repeat until each match is made. Do you understand?"

"Yes," I say once again, my voice a small roar among a crowd of eager cheers. Every muscle in my body stands out in sharp relief, rage and indignation rendering them solid.

I swear to the end of the world and beyond, I will *destroy this place and all the men who've condoned it.*

"Fantastic." Lucian smiles. "Before retiring to your accommodations tonight, you'll be asked to sign a document at the door. It's your sworn agreement to these rules, a violation of which will remove you from your elite stature and exclude you from all auctions moving forward. Depending on the severity of your violation, further punishment may also be deemed appropriate."

He nods toward the door, where his assistant stands and gestures for everyone to take note before we're escorted out to our accommodations—otherwise known as the châteaus scattered across the far side of the property, each at least a mile away.

In addition to the sworn contracts we're forced to sign, the Elite Council goes to great lengths to keep us separated from the women's scents at night. Each of us is assigned one of the châteaus as a private residence for the duration of our stay.

It's also where the bonding night festivities are meant to take place.

After that comes a polite little goodbye breakfast the following morning, where we're expected to leave the estate with our new women and return to our lives in the real world.

"Good. Now I'd like to welcome Max Gustav up here to say a few words of thanks to the men who've made this possible."

My uncle steps aside, and Max whoeverthefuck takes the floor, pulling a sheet of paper from his pocket to read a list of names like this is some sort of governmental press conference at the scene of a national disaster.

He hems and haws, and I close my eyes to log each and every name on my growing hit list.

Joseph Froth.

William Aster.

Hoyt Carson.

Lucian Wrath.

The list carries on for well over a minute before the president of the Council, Narris Novak, steps forward once again.

"Thank you, Max. Lucian. Gentlemen of the Council, and all of you here tonight—"

I jolt as a voice I recognize overpowers the ass-kissing being done by the president of the Elite Council and takes over my awareness.

"Cal, are you there? Can you hear me with those big-ass ears of yours, or did they cut them off?"

Relief, swift and unrelenting, hits me square in the face at the sound of Kane, my clowning, taunting, always playing brother...alive and well and talking directly to me using one of the only advantages we have—my super hearing. If I were with him right now, I'd kiss him on the lips for thinking of it.

The only problem, of course, is that my ability to listen doesn't help at all with the part where I'm supposed to be answering him back.

I listen harder, hoping he'll keep going without getting an answer from me. "Yes, Rook, I know. Relax. I'm getting to it," Kane says. It'd be annoying to listen to their bickering right now if it weren't so good to know that they're together, *alive*, and sounding so much like themselves I could yell.

I don't know if that's by design or if they've managed to sneak a visit, but either way, it's a small victory in an ever-deepening cesspool of bad news.

"Rook says to invite him into your mind," Kane instructs.

Rook, I think.

"Okay, Rook says he can hear you." Kane laughs. "Though,

he says it'd be helpful if you thought about more than his name."

"I didn't say that," Rook argues verbally with Kane.

"Yeah, but I could tell by the way you looked at me, you were thinking it," Kane blathers on.

Rook, please, I interrupt again. *Kind of multitasking right now, so it'd be great if we got to the point.*

"Cal would like us to get to the point," Rook tells Kane, which only makes him laugh.

"Right. Yeah. Well, there isn't much of one…yet. I guess. We just wanted to see if we could get in touch with you and check that you were all right. Are you…all right?"

Fucking miserable and disgusted and crawling out of my skin, I answer. *But yes. I'm fine.*

"Good. We're fine too. Bored as fuck and under lock and key, but fine. Kylie and Blair are hanging in there too."

At the thought of their mates temporarily safe behind their protection and a locked door, all I can think of is my own. *Romy.*

Left to fend for herself while I fight the demons on this side of the mirror. I could tell by the look on her face and the posture of her body tonight that she's terrified. Unlike many of the women here, she can sense the danger of the situation, and her trepidation only grows the longer the process goes on. I can only imagine how frightening it felt to be locked into her room tonight, and I wish I could comfort her or send her some sort of—

"Who's Romy?" Rook asks, startling me violently into

my own brain. I immediately slam the door shut on our connection.

I'd like to use the excuse that I'm not used to having someone inside my thoughts as the reason for my slip of consciousness, but it was a rookie move at best. And with the stakes as high as they are these days, I need to be better.

I need to be on my fucking game, day in and day out.

"Romy? What do you mean, who's Romy?" Kane asks excitedly.

I sigh heavily, trying to rein myself in when my uncle's eyes land on me from the front of the room. He's watching me closely, and for the first time, I consider the idea that he might have some ability to read my thoughts or my intentions like my brothers. He already proved in our cabin in Connecticut that his powers go far beyond those considered normal. I don't know if I could stop him if he can, but that doesn't mean I won't try.

Locking my brain in fortitude and metal bars and concrete walls, I shield myself with heavy armor and blind hope.

"Cal. His thoughts. He's worried about *Romy*," Rook explains to Kane as I listen, relaxing my shoulders and loosening my jaw for the sake of my uncle.

"Ah, fuck, Cal," Kane says, his voice annoyingly sympathetic. "It happened, didn't it? It fucking clicked for you too. You saw your mate…oh wait…*fuck*. Your mate is in there? At the fucking auction? Oh, holy hell, and I thought Blair and I had shitty timing…"

I don't answer, of course. Not only can I not, I don't have

to. They know—just like they knew for themselves. The universe has spoken, and there's no going back.

"Fuck, man." Rook is in my ear now. "I'm…sorry. Sorry that it's happening like this, where you're going to have to fight it so hard. But just…don't do anything stupid, okay? We really can't afford to have shit going even more off the rails than it already is."

Yeah, I know, Rook, I open up my mind to him once more.

It's all the confirmation I'll give. The only concession I'll make.

Because like it or not—Romy is the reason for my every move now, and saving this group of women from the fate of all the women before them is even more important.

She's the key to my personal drive, and in all likelihood, the reason I'll succeed.

The universe designed it that way.

Because when it comes to Romy Spencer, there's no other option.

I won't fail. I can't.

9

ROMY

ITH MY MAKEUP REMOVED AND MY dress discarded to a pile in the corner of my room, I pick up the schedule Abigail gave me on the way to our rooms from my nightstand and take it with me to the high-backed, floral-upholstered chair to read through it.

It's not that I don't know the gist—*flounce around so vampires can window-shop, hit the auction block while vampires purchase, lie down in a skimpy outfit while said vampire uses blood supply and maybe my body, and then perhaps, or maybe not if I'm lucky, die.*

It's the detailed layout I've been avoiding up until now on the premise of stupidly maintaining some semblance of sanity, but after being surprised tonight by the montage and Cal and the skimpy wardrobe selection, I think I have to switch tactics to a more *knowledge-is-power* approach.

After clicking on the floor lamp at the side to combat the moody lighting—the decor in general is very Dracula's lair coded with dark colors, creepy florals, and low visibility—I tuck my bare knees into the front of my oversized T-shirt and stick my nose inside the collar for comfort. It smells like me and home and life before the world tilted to the vampire-centric axis.

Slowly but carefully, I read through the itinerary, shivering lightly as each item gets more frightening than the last.

Arrival Day

6:15 p.m. Welcome Mixer in Ground Floor Ballroom (Dress to Impress)

8:15 p.m. Return to Rooms for Rest and Recharge

Day 2

8:30 a.m. Room Service Breakfast

10:00 a.m. Individual Fitness/Meditation Time

12:00 Lunch Buffet on South Terrace

2:00 p.m. Mini Spa in Multipurpose Room

6:15 p.m. Co-Ed Mixer in Ground Floor Ballroom (Dress to Impress)

Day 3

8:30 a.m. Room Service Breakfast

10:00 a.m. Individual Fitness/Meditation Time

12:00 Lunch Buffet on South Terrace

3:00 p.m. Hair and Makeup in Ground Floor Ballroom

6:00 p.m. Official Selection

8:00 p.m. Couples Ceremony

10:00 p.m. Bonding Night

My hand trembles as I set the schedule down on the side table next to the chair, marveling at their ability to make it sound like an expensive retreat or spa experience rather than what it is—a freaking wholesale market for humans.

"Unbelievable."

Desperate for a distraction or, perhaps, a hidden pickaxe like the one Andy Dufresne used to escape in *The Shawshank Redemption*, I thumb through the spines of the books they have stacked next to the lamp, settling on one halfway down when the title stops me in my tracks.

VAMPIRE SERVITUDE: DESTINY OR DYNASTY

Okay, yikes.

I flip open the front cover to a picture of a man and his biography—a vampire, obviously—and roll my eyes as he starts mansplaining a woman's role in their relationship before the book even starts.

Harrow Rostakov is an award-winning vampire-human relations specialist with sixty years of experience decoding the human woman's mind. Known for his accomplishments in the Selection acclimation space, Rostakov has successfully transitioned over a thousand women into their new purpose of servitude and unlocked the power of their family's dynasty as the game-changing motivation.

It's the epitome of narcissism to think you know best about an experience you haven't actually lived and reminds me of the arrogant male gynecologist my mother took me to for my first appointment at fifteen years old. He negated pain, belittled the woman's cycle, and presumed to know more about my uterus from reading a book than I did by living with it.

Don't get me wrong; there are men out there who *aren't* like that, but they're few and far between at best. I highly doubt they're congregating in record numbers at a market for blood-appropriate women.

Slamming the book shut and picking up the next, **The First-Time High**, I select a paragraph to read about the bonding night.

As soon as the words *fang* and *blood* make their debut, I toss it back to the pile, turn off the overhead light, and head for the bed.

There are no tools inside these books—only horror stories.

Conversely, one of the only boons of this little adventure is the luxurious bedding, so I may as well get some rest and relaxation while taking advantage of it. Clearly, tomorrow's got a full damn schedule, and I doubt they take kindly to the idea of skipping it to stay barricaded in your room. My guard, in particular, looks as though he'd delight in dragging me around the mansion by my shiny red hair if needed.

Flopping hard, I roll to my side and tuck a hand under my pillow before exhaling dramatically.

I still cannot believe my parents—the people who spent their lives and time and energy raising me—have sent me off to be sold to a freaking vampire just so our family legacy can stay intact. I've tried to put myself in their position and see it from their side, but this thing is one-dimensional as shit.

Selling humans equals bad. Period.

Ugh.

Closing my eyes, I inhale deeply to suck the lavender of the linen to the back of my nostrils and, if possible, my brain. It's a calming scent innately, but I'm afraid, under these circumstances, it's got its work cut out for it.

The longer I lie there, the more depressing the darkness of my confinement feels. It's silent, save a solitary ticking noise I can't place, that comes and goes every ten seconds or so, and with that comes a myriad of unblocked, unchecked, wholly distressing thoughts.

How scared I am.

How nothing I've ever known—not even my childhood crush on the nicest boy in school—seems safe.

How hopeless I feel against a power so much greater than me.

How lacking in support I am, even from the people who're supposed to love me most.

A single tear escapes my closed eyes, and I wipe it away frantically before squeezing them shut tighter. My ears whoosh with the effort to close everything but sleep out, but the noise persists.

When I find myself counting along to its rhythm instead of drifting off to a numbing slumber, I cover my ear with my hand. But it's like a dripping faucet—impossible to ignore.

Rolling to my back, I stare at the ceiling and will it to go away. It doesn't.

I groan.

Instead, it gets faster the longer I disregard it, and, finally, frustrated enough by the incessance, I throw back the large comforter and pull the string on the lamp at my bedside to turn it back on.

As the sound grows, I climb from the bed and trudge toward it, pausing in front of the armoire on the wall when the sound gets louder. Shaking slightly, I pull the brass knob on the door to open the cabinet, fearing the worst inside—like a ghost or a demon or, I don't know, a portal to the next dimension. I know it's farfetched, but it's hard to imagine a bottom to the well of possibility when I'm already dealing in freaking vampires, for Pete's sake.

Chalk it up to the new digs, but my brain is firmly in nightmare territory every time it tries to make something up.

The armoire is empty, though, save a plush black robe and two extra pillows, and after a quick shuffle of the contents with my hand, unfortunately, the noise persists.

What the hell is that?

I move to the side of the cabinet and press my head to the wall to take a look behind it, and when a sliver of silver light hits me square in the eye, I jump.

Oh my God. Is that…is that a window?

I haven't seen the outside in six, maybe seven, hours, and even then, it was a rushed jog from the car to the front door upon arrival.

I could go for a big gulp of real air right now—or maybe, a shimmy down my sheets and an Olympic sprint to somewhere, anywhere, else.

Leaning my shoulder into the dark, rich wood, I push as hard as I can in an attempt to move the heavy cabinet to the side, but the only thing that slides is me.

I pull off my socks and chuck them toward the bed, getting a running start and slamming my shoulder into the wood once again. If there's anything that could renew my determination and sheer strength of will, it's the possibility of escape, and a window at this point is practically a portal to another dimension.

Being given the room at the end of the hall might just be the stroke of good luck I've been waiting for.

Momentum finally builds as I push with every ounce of energy I have left, and I churn my feet like I'm sprinting, even though I'm moving no more than inches at a time. As the cabinet slides,

I push harder, groaning slightly when it's finally far enough over to bring the window into view. A blackout blind is down, and I pull the cord at the side to open it, wincing slightly as it whines.

I watch the door from my spot behind the cabinet, just waiting for my guard to bust through it like a battering ram. I only breathe again when the shade is out of place completely and the door is still closed.

Pressing my forehead to the glass, I peer out into the silver darkness of the new-moon night, trying to find the source of the noise or a feasible way down to ground level.

When a face pops up in front of mine, I scream.

Shit!

As Calloway Slater's features come into focus, I smother the rest of my outburst with a hand over my mouth on sheer instinct, and I fight against an actively panicking heart.

The damage is already done, however. A scream during quiet hours isn't the kind of thing these vampires are going to shrug off, I imagine.

"Hey!" my guard yells. "What's going on in there?"

Shit, shit, shit. If they find me over here with the cabinet moved and my window open, I don't even want to think about what they'll do or where they'll move me instead.

Three harsh knocks ring out from my door, and with no other option, I run over to it on fast feet.

Taking a deep breath and steeling my nerves, I pull it open just enough to peek my head out and immediately start apologizing. "Sorry. So sorry. I was reading and fell asleep and went straight into a nightmare where I was falling off a cliff after being shoved! Then there was a…a train in the ocean…headed right for me…

and holy hell, it blared its horn and I screamed, but I was actually awake then, and the next thing I know, I'm sitting up in bed screaming and you're knocking."

My guard's eyebrows draw together as he works to follow my nonsense.

"A nightmare?" he eventually asks.

"Yes. It was awful. But I'm good now, so you can lock me back up and go back to keeping guard out here."

"Maybe I'll just come in—"

"No!" I'm quick to cut him off. "I'm very sloppy, and I have underwear and private things all over the place. No." Calming myself slightly, I tone my voice to something less commanding. I doubt my guard likes a woman trying to tell him what to do either. "No. Thank you. You don't need to come in. I'm good, I swear. No more screams."

When he doesn't close it immediately, I pull it out of his grip and do it for him, turning the lock on the inside of the knob for good measure. I know he has a key, and that no silly lock on my side of the door is going to keep my vampire guard out of my room if he wants in it anyway, but it's more about the symbolism than anything else.

I wait five full seconds after I'm done, my ear pressed against the wood to listen for more movement on his end, but when I don't hear anything, I run straight back to the window and jump into action to figure out how to get it open.

In addition to the latch, there's another lock at the side, but I engage my spidey-moves and climb the edge of the armoire with sweaty feet to reach it.

Shoving from the bottom as hard as I can to break the

dried-over paint, I jump when Cal's face invades mine. "Back up," he whispers, pushing me gently.

This isn't the worried, timid Cal I saw tonight in the hallway. This is a man on a mission.

What the mission is, I fear I don't know.

When he's through the opening, I scurry back, leaning out into the breeze to get a look at the surroundings, expecting to find a ladder or a trellis or something. But all I find is open space and the textured stone of the side of the building.

No stairs. No rope. No tied-together bedsheets or the like, and absolutely none of the other escape-scenario tools I imagined.

"How the hell did you get up here?" I ask incredulously.

Cal moves me out of the way before closing the window with a finger to his lips—a warning to lower my voice, no doubt—and the burn of his hands on my arms lingers long after he lets go.

When I stare at my skin to see if there's an accompanying glow, I catch sight of the peak of my nipples, and my very braless state comes roaring back into focus. I cross my arms over my chest self-consciously and squeeze my thighs together to limit the very noticeable flow of air.

Suddenly, the big T-shirt and panties as sleep attire is feeling a little vulnerable.

Cal's figure cuts an imposing shadow as he scans the room around us, getting a feel for the layout and assuring himself it's just him and me alone. His jaw is carved in hard lines, and his eyes look wildly blue even in the dim light of the deep green walls.

When his harsh gaze cuts to me, my whole chest expands.

He doesn't look like he's dropped by for a friendly visit—he looks *consumed*. For the first time since he appeared at my window, I have the good sense to be scared of *him*.

I want to believe he's here as some sort of knight in shining armor, but the truth is, he could just as easily be here to hurt me.

"Cal. What are you doing here?" This time, it's a whisper and a plea. I didn't realize how on the very edge of fucking losing my careful hold on rationality I was until the rock started to crumble beneath me.

He sighs, running a jagged hand through his perfect brown hair. "I don't know." He paces from one square of carpet to the next and back again, chuckling ever so lightly.

"Was that…" I shake my head, trying to dislodge the shock and confusion of having him here in my room. Of having *this* up close and personal. "You making that tapping noise?"

"Yeah." He runs a hand through his hair before letting out a deep sigh. "And, Romy, the fact is, I don't know what the hell I'm doing here. I shouldn't be. I know that beyond a shadow of a doubt. But I *needed* to see you. Needed…to talk. After running into you in the hall tonight, I just had to come. I couldn't leave things the way we did, leave you thinking I'm…one of these men."

I nod, unsure of what to say. Rubbing my lips together and then licking to wet them because of my nerves, I watch as his eyes fall to the movement and snag.

My awareness ratchets up to an eleven as a pool of arousal fills in my abdomen. It's ill-timed and at odds with my nerves, but it's there. So much so, it feels unrelenting.

"Okay…" I force myself to focus. "So…what?" I hold out both hands. "What do you want to explain? Because the question I can't seem to come up with an answer for is at odds with what you're saying. If you're not *one of these men*, what are you doing here, Cal?" I shake my head, willing myself to take my time to find the words I need to make sense. "I don't just mean my room. But *here*. At this place with these…men. I mean…you're a *vampire?*"

He nods, and I swallow.

"Like…you've always been? Even when we were kids?"

He nods again. "We're born. Not created or turned or…whatever the fuck else fiction makes it out to be. It's not allowed. At least, not legally. I've been what I am since my very first cry."

"So, your brothers are—"

"Vampires too," he confirms before clearing his throat.

"Are they here?"

"Sort of." His smile is both sad and confusing. Quite frankly, it's everything a smile shouldn't be, and I hate the look of it on his handsome face. "It's a long story."

"Well, I don't know how much time we have before I jump out the window and run away, but why don't you start at the beginning, and we'll take it from there? If I'm gone in the middle, you can finish telling it to the spot where I used to be."

His smile turns soft as he moves to my bed and sits down at the foot of it, offering the spot under the covers to me with a gesture of his hand.

I want to stand in revolt, but a sudden bout of sheer exhaustion makes me take him up on the offer. I sit on the bed and inhale slightly when he places the cover over my legs with the gentleness of someone a quarter of his size. And because I'm completely unhinged, I find myself wishing he'd cover me with his body instead.

What on earth is wrong with me?

"Running isn't a good idea, Romy. I wish it were, but I promise, they'd catch you."

I sigh. "Yeah. I was afraid of that."

"So…how've you been?"

The ironically simplistic question makes me laugh, and because he's earned my compliance with his gentled approach, I make sure to do it quietly. "Well…not bad until a couple of days ago. Can't say I'm thrilled with the current trajectory, but it's hardly a surprise. My parents have been talking about the selection since I was a toddler."

He nods. "If it makes you feel any better, I haven't had the best week either. Lots of ups and downs and ultimatums I don't really like."

I worry my lip with my teeth, trying to make sense of the Cal I knew—the one who seems to be in front of me now—and the kind of Cal he would have to be to be a part of something like this and how they could possibly fit together to make one man. "Is that why you're here? Because of an ultimatum?"

"It's more complicated than that, but yes, sort of. It wasn't the only option, but it was the best one." He rubs a hand over his own knee, the rest of him frozen in deep thought. "I'm here because I'm seeking change. I'm here for my brothers and their mates, and I'm here… Well, I'm here for you."

"For *me*?" My stomach tightens, and my back plasters to the headboard, knowing I'm cooked if he turns out to be dangerous. There's no way I'd get out of this bed in time, but I guess I could say the same for any position I'd take in this room.

Vampires are so physically superior, it's not even funny.

"I know that sounds…ominous," he confirms with a gentle

nod and an even gentler face. "And I promise I'll explain when I can. Just know…" He places a hand to his chest I swear I feel as though he's laid it upon my own. "I would never hurt you, Romy. More than that—I would kill anyone else who tried."

My throat burns as I swallow his words. They're bold. They're romantic.

They're *terrifying*.

10

CAL

H AIR DOWN AND FACE FLUSHED, ROMY SPENCER is the picture of every fantasy I never had for a mate but absolutely would have if I'd ever allowed myself to consider the possibility of love. She's naturally beautiful, funny, and intelligence radiates from every speck of her worried blue eyes.

Coming here was a risk in every sense of the word—with the Elite Council, with my uncle, and maybe most dangerously, with her.

With temptation, of course, but more importantly, with landing myself a spot in her favor.

Destiny only gets you so far when the woman is scared of you, and I know by declaring my intentions just now, I've stacked the deck against myself even higher.

But this isn't the time for timid plans and managed expectations. This is the last-chance, Hail Mary throw right at the precipice of death.

I either win now or lose for everyone.

And I've never, ever liked losing as an option.

"I know that sounds…ominous," I hedge carefully, posturing myself as a man who understands her position, though I know I never truly will. "And I promise I'll explain when I can." I want to reach out and touch her—to steady her with the righteousness of my intent. But I carry that to my own chest with a splayed hand instead, gripping at my heart and willing it to show itself in the tone of my voice. "Just know…I would never hurt you, Romy. More than that—I would kill anyone else who tried."

Romy's body folds on itself as the reality of how invested I am in her comes to a head in her mind. The obsession. The primality. The whole premise of a mate and its unbreakable need for its other half.

It's foreign to her in ways I can't even begin to comprehend and probably scary in half a dozen others. But I didn't stop myself from coming here tonight. And I didn't stop myself from tapping on her window. Didn't stop myself from climbing through said window. And I definitely didn't stop myself from sitting here on her bed.

And because of all those failures in control, I have no choice but to give it to her as honestly as prioritizing her safety will allow.

She swallows thickly, and I look down, hoping to offer her the space and comfort to ask more questions—to ask me whatever she wants. It takes her a minute of silence and the comfort of my best impression of a statue, but eventually, she finds the courage to challenge me for more information.

"Is…killing someone for me something that might be necessary, say, soon?"

"I hope not," I say. It's a lie, but it's the answer she needs both from the man she wants to trust and for the fear she's already battling. "But for you, for my brothers, I wouldn't hesitate."

"Your brothers. Yeah…you said before… You said your brothers *and* their…mates."

"Yes," I confirm. "My brothers have both mated already. I have not. I know it's confusing with the selection process you see here, but biologically, vampires are meant for only one human mate. Their fated mate. It's not a choice or a bidding war—it's destiny. Some of the men here don't think that's how it should be."

"Is that why you're here? Looking for her? Your…fated mate?"

I shake my head, smoothing the edges of an answer she already knows. "I don't need to look." I smile sensitively. "Not outside of this room, at least."

Her nervous laugh is consciously quiet of the guard in the hall but out of hand at the same time. Her control of her fear is rattled, and I know it's unlikely she can handle much more.

"So, you're saying I… That I'm your…" Eyes wide and hands shaking, she clenches the comforter in her lap.

"I know it might be startling for you, but I knew the moment I saw you tonight." I pause. "*Intrinsically.*"

Surprising me entirely, her face softens in understanding, and the tension in her shoulders sinks with a renewing ease. I thought she'd be scrambling for safety right now.

"Is that…is *that* why I've been feeling this way since I ran into you outside the bathroom?"

"What is *this way*? How do you feel?"

"Unsettled," she says simply, her eyes finding the ceiling as she searches for the most accurate words. "Somewhat frantic. I mean, I haven't felt really great about the whole thing altogether, but since I saw you, I've felt…antsy. Until now. Right now, I feel… calm."

Calm.

The word strikes me like a lightning bolt.

My gaze drops to her mouth before I can stop it, taking in the soft curve of her lips and the way her breath catches slightly between words.

And something low and instinctive pulls tight in my chest.

Mine. Romy Spencer is *mine.*

The urge to close the distance between us is immediate and fucking overwhelming. My body already leans forward before my mind catches up, before I remember where we are. Before I remember what this is.

I force myself still, dragging in a slow breath and anchoring my hands at my sides so I don't reach for her.

"There's a reason I went to the bathroom when I did," I say. "A reason I came here even though it's expressly forbidden and scaled the wall to get up here. There's a *reason*. A reason so much bigger than I've ever understood before now. A reason bigger than me or you or the people on this estate who think they're above it."

"*Cal.*" My eyes shutter as the voice in front of me shifts to another inside my head. Romy's lips don't move because she's not said a word. Intrusively, Kane repeats my name. "Cal. Can you hear me?"

I open my mind to Rook, my thoughts preemptively loaded with annoyance and their shit timing, and his answer is to chuckle loudly.

"Oh, man," Kane interjects. "You made Rook laugh. Like,

really laugh. I can only fucking imagine what you must be thinking."

"Cal?" Romy asks, confused by the distant haze of my eyes and stagnation of our conversation.

"Sorry," I apologize, shutting Rook out of my mind immediately.

"Hey, what the fuck? Why the hell are you shutting us out?" Kane complains, but I ignore him.

"I'm sorry. Did you ask me something?" Romy is my only focus right now. Every minute I spend in this room and not in my château is a risk to both of us. As much as I wish we did, we don't have a lot of time.

"I asked if you're okay with what's happening here?" she questions. "Because I want to believe you're the guy I used to know, and I want to believe that there's some kind of magical, romantic fate that's pulling us together as…*mates*, but I am so busy freaking the hell out about this…*place* and the way they're—"

"I hate this place," I say, cutting her off gently. My voice rumbles with the gravel of all the bullshit that's brought us here. "This *tradition*. I hate it with every physical fiber of my being and the theoretical beyond. Romy, I promise you…I would never, *ever* be here if I didn't have to be. And I want to explain that to you in detail, to put your mind at ease in any way I can, but I can't right now because there are too many variables and too many risks." I sigh. "I know it's selfish and demanding. But I need you to trust me blindly. I need you to feel this thing between us and give in to it if you can. I need you—"

"I…I will. I do. Trust you."

I freeze, overwhelmed by her unexpected submission and how wholly it touches me.

"Maybe it's naïve of me," she continues, "or maybe I'm just out of options, but Cal…seeing you in that hall tonight gave me the first full breath I've had in forty-eight hours. Hell, probably the first full breath I've had in *years*. And seeing you here, in my room, is the best I've felt in a long time. I don't understand it, but given the alternative, I don't need to." She shrugs. "I'm going all in on my instincts. For the guy I had a crush on when we were kids. I'm going all in for the guy who says he'd kill someone for me, all in on the kind of romance I never thought I'd get, and all in for one last chance to ruin my mother's day. Because let me tell you, she is going to *hate* this."

Without thought or pause or restraint or the ability to hold myself back anymore, I lean forward and kiss her.

It's a slow, closed-mouth kiss until she finds my neck with her hands and squeezes, and then I can't help but breach the seam of her lips with my tongue and take a full taste.

She's shooting stars and the lunar eclipse and validation for all the risks I've taken to get here. She's strawberries and sweet cream, and memories of a childhood in a parallel universe. She's the answer to my questions and the reason I don't ask why and, despite not knowing how badly I needed it, she's the renewed fire under my ass to take this place apart one fucking screw at a time.

When I pull back, there's only one word left to say. "*Fuck.*"

Shoving off the bed, I take to pacing beside it.

The longing to complete the bonding engulfs me, the smell of her blood and her pussy so distinct I'll never forget it, and my need rages from the tip of my toes to the top of my head, a visceral reaction I can't control.

But it's too much for now—for her to handle and for the risk it creates of discovery by the guard outside her room, my uncle, or the Council itself.

Romy's eyes are wide and her mouth flushed as she pushes herself up against the headboard again, no doubt frightened by my frenzy. I take a step away and steady my voice. "Push the armoire back in front of the window after I leave," I instruct, and she nods.

I charge toward the window, desperate for the relief of Romy-scent-free air and labored by the repeated knocks inside my mind from both Kane and Rook. They're fighting to break my grip, and I know I won't be able to hold them off much longer.

But I'll be damned if I'm going to let them in while I'm still here—while I'm feeling like this.

Romy follows behind me on her toes, her tanned legs feeling forever long as they peek out from under her sleep shirt. Her pretty auburn hair is ruffled, and I want to sink my hands into the roots of it so badly it hurts.

"Tomorrow, if you can, try to build some mistrust in the women," I tell her. "Nothing huge or obvious. Just little seeds of doubt."

She snorts. "Oh, no problem there. I'm already on the case. I've been complaining about this farce of an honor since the moment they met me."

"Romy?"

"Yeah?"

"Thanks for trusting me. I won't betray it. I promise."

This time, she's the one to lean forward and take my mouth

with hers. Indulging slightly, I sink a hand into her hair and savor the moment. Soft tendrils feel like silk, and her mouth feels like home. The pull to stay grows and stings so much it might scar.

My brothers' kidnappings of their fated mates are suddenly making a hell of a lot more sense.

Breaking contact while I still can, I climb out the window and wait just below it until I'm sure Romy has it relocked. Once on the ground, I watch until the light from the room disappears, indicating that she's managed to get the cabinet back in its place, and then stalk through the dark with both speed and finesse.

Crickets chirp as I make my way through the garden and past the fountain to the stretch of wooded gravel path that leads to each of the attending vampires' châteaus. I take to the trees instead of staying out in the open, carefully listening for any of them to ensure they haven't noticed me as I make the mile-long trek.

Kane and Rook still beat at my brain, but I don't allow either of them in until I'm back inside my own villa for the night, with the door closed behind me.

"Hey, fucker. How's it feel to be as stupid as the rest of us? Because I know you're doing something you shouldn't—"

"Kane, stop. He let me in again," Rook interrupts.

I sigh. *You rang?*

"Wow, Cal," Kane says with a groan. "A little space from us and you're turning into a real smartass. These elite fucks aren't bleeding into you, are they?"

Don't even fucking joke.

"Easy, Kane," Rook warns. "You remember how you felt in the early stages of the bond, don't you?"

"Fuck talking about the bond," I demand, touchy on the

subject after being forced to leave Romy behind in her room, to say the least. I feel like I'm suffocating, and I don't even need air to fucking breathe. It hurts too bad. I feel crazy inside my own skin.

I tug at my shirt collar, and when that's not enough, I pull it off with a hand between my shoulders, tossing it to the sofa and pacing. *I'm handling the bond. I wanna talk about how the fuck we're going to dismantle this thing piece by piece until it'll never be built again. I want to talk about how much fucking pain we're going to make them feel. I want to talk about murder.*

"Okay, yikes. Didn't mean to push on a nerve," Kane apologizes snarkily.

I growl.

"We were kind of hoping you'd have some direction, Cal," Kane says, changing his tone to a much gentler vibe. "You're the demolition man after all."

"They've got us locked in this villa, bud, so we're a little short on information," Rook adds. "All we can do is fuck and, well, fight with each other. It's not a bad deal, but—"

Forget it. I'll figure it out myself, I say it to them and myself.

"Whoa, whoa, now calm down," Kane hedges. "We're not saying that. We're just saying we need more information. We need tasks. We need to see you."

All right, I agree. *I'll find a way to get to you tomorrow.*

"We'll be waiting."

I'm not certain about a lot of shit, but I am certain about this—plan or no fucking plan, we end this.

Plan or no fucking plan, Romy will walk away from this alive.

11

GROGGINESS CLINGS TO ME AS A KNOCK ON MY door wakes me from a hard slumber. I glance to the armoire first, half expecting it to open its own doors to Narnia or Cal or some other dreamlike fantasy, but when the knock sounds again, I realize it's coming from the actual door.

Two questions hit me instantly. *What time is it*, and *how the hell much did I drink last night?*

I jump from the bed and run to my suitcase first, climbing into a pair of shorts like I'm in a timed Olympic sport, and then scurry to the door as the fist meets its wood for a third time—third time may normally be the charm, but this time, it's just more demanding.

My guard waits with a tray of breakfast foods as I pull it open, an annoyed impatience crinkling his face. He's handsome for the most part, but a much too heavy brow and a pucker around imaginary sour grapes are ruining the balance of his features.

"Sorry," I apologize, the habit of minimizing my basic human needs so ingrained in me from birth that I'm literally coddling my captor. "I…was asleep."

He extends the tray of food instead of replying, so I accept it in kind and close the door without another word, mocking grumpy puss's face with a comical scrunch of my own as I do.

The childish gesture is an uninvited reminder of my mother's betrayal, and all at once, I'm angry again.

But it's not the quiet, simmering kind of anger. It's the kind that claws its way up your throat and demands to be acknowledged.

My mother didn't just *let* this happen—she *prepared* me for it. She made sure my bags were packed like I was going off to summer camp instead of being handed over on a silver platter of expensive gowns and designer shoes.

And there wasn't a single time when she showcased any concern for my well-being—any care for me at all.

My jaw tightens as I set the tray down harder than necessary.

The amount of therapy I'll probably need when this is over—*if* I even survive it—won't be solved through those apps where you can text with a therapist. Hypnotherapy, damn near daily sessions, I'm going to need all the bells and whistles. At the very least, a punch card situation—*buy ten emotional breakdowns, get one free.*

Still, for as many faults as this place has, the smell of the food isn't one of them, and my deference for alcohol over sustenance last night rears its ugly head in the form of a stomach growl.

After setting the tray down on the side table by the chair, I plop into the floral fabric and fall over the breakfast bits like a vulture. First the eggs and then the fruit, and I finish by tearing into the pastry with my hands until it's completely pulled apart and in my mouth.

The softness of the bread melts like cotton candy on my tongue in direct disagreement with the barbaric way I've consumed it, and I hate that it's given me even an ounce of enjoyment. This place is not an all-inclusive vacay—this place is evil incarnate.

Immediate needs met, I gulp down an entire glass of juice and set it back on the tray and then move to the armoire on the far wall to perform an inspection as the mystery of my mind comes to a head.

Since sleeping, the details of last night have fogged a bit, and I find myself wondering if the little girl who used to chase Calloway Slater around on the playground consorted with the scared woman staring down the barrel of this auction's gun to manifest a better option in the form of a dream.

And maybe, just maybe, Cal didn't scale a plain stone wall to climb in my window last night and declare himself as my *fated mate* after all.

Perhaps I put my head to pillow in the middle of a plush, luxurious bed of fine linens and fell fast asleep and into the clutches of vivid REM-driven fantasy.

It'd be sad. Devastating, even. But it'd make a hell of a lot more sense.

Moving to the side of the armoire, I lean my shoulder into it and try to push. It doesn't budge, as suspected, and a certain sense of deflation makes my stomach feel queasy.

I mean, I knew my recollection of events seemed farfetched, but…*could I really have dreamed that whole damn thing?*

My fingers go instinctively to my lips, touching them gently. Warmth radiates there, and the overwhelming sense that it's not from the eggs begs me to believe it.

If that kiss wasn't real, I'm very good at fantasizing.

Spinning slowly, I put my shoulder to the cabinet again, but this time, I imagine Cal on the other side of the window calling to me. It takes me a few seconds and a lot of muscle, but the cabinet starts to move.

I stop abruptly as the raw certainty that last night was *not* a dream at all takes over.

I'm not crazy.

I *know* Cal was here.

I *know* how his lips felt on mine.

I *know* the completeness that knitted the very gap I feel now in my chest.

I *know*.

And with that certainty, I gain more of my memory.

His explanation of our destiny. His war with himself over being here. His simple request that I seed the doubt of the women alongside me and his belief in my ability to do it without calling attention to myself.

He wasn't just here. He was the answer to my prayers and the savior I've always dreamed of. He was the man of integrity I so desperately wanted him to be, and he was the affirmation my instincts needed.

As a plan hatches within my mind, I double-check the schedule for my next move.

10:00 a.m. Individual Fitness/Meditation Time

And then, I search my bag for workout clothes.

It's not about the fitness—it's about the opportunity to mingle. Without a phone or computer or any access to the other girls or their rooms, the scheduled activities are the only way to make waves.

And at Cal's specific request, make waves I will.

12

CAL

ROMY IS THE FIRST THING ON MY MIND WHEN I wake up.

She was the last thing there when I fell asleep too—memories of the kiss we shared front and center in my mind.

And that memory hasn't loosened its grip on me for a second since.

Being separated from her in a place like this—where danger lurks behind every polished door and smiling face—has my nerves pulled tighter than I'd like to admit.

The bond is growing by the minute. I can feel it. A steady pull in my chest that deepens with every hour we're kept apart. My body is already seeking her out, already craving the closeness that watching my brothers find their mates taught me to recognize for what it is.

I rinse the last of the shaving cream from my face, beads of water clinging to my skin, just as a knock sounds at the door, interrupting the process of getting ready for breakfast.

The schedule for Selection members isn't as detailed as the one they've built for the ladies, but it's enough to keep us busy most hours of the day. I recognize it for what it is—control—but dread it for another reason entirely.

At this point, every moment spent away from Romy burns a deeper pit into my stomach.

I wipe my face with the towel by the sink, grab the dress shirt draped over the foot of the bed, and sling it over my shoulders as I move toward the door. My fingers work through the buttons automatically while I cross the room at a speed that would blur for human eyes.

Lucian's smirk is pointed and assessing as I open the door.

Keeping me off-kilter and unable to plan is a strategy I recognize all too well from several of the foster homes my brothers and I found ourselves in growing up. It's weakness assessment in its most innocent form, but unfortunately for my uncle, I'm even better at the game.

I've had to be.

"Good morning, Lucian," I greet, my words echoing the confidence of my posture. "I've been expecting you."

"You have?" A grin tilts the corner of his mouth, but the sinister nature of the curvature is far from a smile.

"Of course."

He assesses me for a long moment before gesturing for me to join him outside, and I pull the door closed behind me as I do just that, tucking my freshly buttoned shirt into my dress pants. It's been a long night of wandering thoughts and incomplete plans, but I find myself more energized than ever at the small victory of catching him off guard.

As a mechanically inclined guy, I know it's the small things like that that can dismantle a whole system's existence. The rubber grommets that hold pressure. The pressure points that support giant spans. I'm one tiny thing away from burning this whole thing to the ground.

And the place to start is at the beginning—*my* beginning.

With my mother.

The woman who gave all three Slater brothers life.

As we stroll the gravel path through the villas, I overturn the first stone. It doesn't matter what his purpose for this morning visit was—now, its purpose is my own. And I want to bleed every ounce of information from him that I can.

"How old was my mother when she came to Selection?"

His pause is minute but noticeable all the same. I log it for later introspection. "She was twenty-two."

"And the vampire who selected her?"

"Nathanial."

I hum. "What made him decide to share her? Pardon my newness to the process and reasoning of the elites, but if I'm to understand it correctly, the whole point of the auction is for the highest bidder to win, is it not?"

"It is," Lucian confirms hesitantly. "But you have to understand that some of the priorities were different back then. The *blood of the four* was, of course, sacred in a way, but there was an assumption of plenty. No worries of replacements and certainly no sense of long-term thinking. It took her being sold off to another group in Rome, dying, and killing off the fourth line for reality to hit home."

Every painful revelation in my poor mother's mistreatment makes me burn hotter. *Shared. Sold. Abused.*

"And…what did it change?" I grit, fighting to maintain control.

He sighs. "For some, nothing. But for the majority, it provided a steadiness to the process. A certain level of decorum and a proprietary level of ownership was born. There is no sharing once bonded anymore, and as a result, we've created a much more… maintainable environment for the women."

I scoff, losing my cool for just a moment. "Maintainable." The word is much more than a sneer. It's an embodiment of disgust and betrayal and a life built on the back of the mistreatment of my mother.

"Yes, Calloway. I know our traditions don't find favorability with you. You've made that clear in a myriad of ways over the last two weeks. But I'm afraid they are the way they are for a reason." He folds his hands together at the small of his back before continuing. "Our culture is born of necessity. As you know, a vampire's needs vary greatly from those of a human. We don't need air or food or sleep. We need power. Precision. Drive. Without these things, survival becomes boring. Basic. Pointless."

I shake my head but bite my tongue.

His description of pointless and my description of it are two ends of a very long stick. The meaning of a vampire's life isn't power—but connection. His *precision* the actual antithesis of the universe's call to comply with it. His *drive* a slap in the face to the mates the fates created for us. Everything he claims we need are the very parts of the puzzle that don't fit.

In fact, it makes us worse and brought us to the brink of ruthlessness.

I want to tell him he's wrong. That every thought he has is an assault on the conscience of a real man. That his *point*, as it were, is my nemesis. But the argument will go nowhere, so I harness the rage this conversation has built for later use instead.

The time *will* come.

For him. For Rook and Kane and our fathers. For all these so-called elites.

"Don't discount it until you've tried it," he says then, stopping in front of a villa at the far end of the property—what must be a mile in the other direction, past the mansion and tucked away in a bed of low shrubbery and woods—and gesturing toward the door.

I won't deny that I've done a piss-poor job of focusing on my surroundings until now, assuming the walk was more of a wander than one to reach a destination, but all engines are firing now. I don't know where he's brought me, and I don't like the possibilities.

That he might know I went to Romy last night. That he knows my connection to her at all.

"Where are we?" I ask, skeptical but collected.

Instead of answering, he raises his cane to the door and knocks before taking a key from the fancy chain at his belt and unlocking the dead bolt.

"See for yourself."

As he walks away, I steel myself for a fight.

An ambush, perhaps. A torture scenario with Romy or my brothers at the center. The Council heads, seated behind a table of entitlement and ready to distribute a judgment of my death.

But when the door opens, it's *Kane* on the other side. Lucian has delivered me directly to my brothers, going so far as to unlock the damn door.

"Cal?" Kane asks, his excitement overwhelming him enough to send him flying into me in a hug.

I return the gesture and spin us to look for Lucian, but he's gone, leaving behind nothing but the wind. I search the woods and the leaves and the piercing light of the sun from just beyond, my uneasiness growing.

This has to be a trap. Or a mind game at the very least.

I don't trust it at all, but beyond that, I don't understand it. Why he would allow me this contact, this boon, this help—I cannot, for the life of me, figure it out. It's manipulation. I wish I knew the goal.

"Rook!" Kane shouts back into the house, the sound of his voice echoing off the walls. "Come here. Now!"

Rook, Kylie, and Blair appear after a few seconds, Rook standing guard in front of the women as though he's explicitly told them not to follow him. It's not a surprise to him that they didn't listen, but it's damn near world-rocking to see me.

So much so, he hits me at a run, challenging Kane's hug for supremacy in every way. It's the most emotion I've seen out of our eldest brother, ever, and I should be overjoyed. Ready to razz him. Basking in the warmth of his emotional maturation.

Instead, I'm on guard. Because I know why he's acting this way—and the reasoning behind it rocks me to my core.

His fear for me—for us and our chances at making it out of this alive—has been far, far greater than he's let on. He wasn't hopeful that we'd make it out of this. Hell, he may have thought he'd never even get to see me again.

"How the fuck did you find us?" Kane asks, pulling Blair

under his arm and tucking her close as she rushes forward to join him.

I shrug. "Lucian." The gesture and the name are a dramatic oversimplification of my feelings on the matter, but the last thing I want to do is alarm Kylie and Blair unnecessarily. They didn't ask for this—these women didn't ask for any of this.

"Lucian?" Rook's question is immediately defensive, and I can't blame him. It's not like our long-lost uncle has been anything short of threatening since we met him in the cabin two days ago, but as Kylie peers over his shoulder, I raise a subtle eyebrow to suggest we really get into it at another time.

"I know," I agree, adding a small detail to hold some of his curiosity at bay. "He showed up at my door this morning and walked me here."

"Who the fuck cares how you got here?" Kane cuts in. "Get your ass inside."

While I do think it's important to work through Lucian bringing me here at a later time, I agree it's a conversation for later. I take the out and step inside.

Rook shuts the door behind me, and we exchange a look at the open dead bolt. They couldn't control it from this side before—but it's unlocked now.

I nod, jerking my chin toward the living room. He presses a hand to Kylie's back, guiding her behind Kane and Blair, and I follow them in.

As soon as my ass hits the cushion on the love seat, I'm yanked back to my feet and pulled into a hug I don't expect.

Kylie's warm breath hits my ear in a rush. "I'm glad you're okay. I've been worried."

"Me too," I reply with a smile, hoping the joke will do the heavy lifting at breaking the tension.

She laughs before rushing back over to the comfort of her mate's arms, and Blair offers me an awkward wave and a smile.

The simple realness of how little we actually know about each other at this stage of a world-changing fight makes me laugh much harder than is appropriate, and the tension in the room ratchets back up.

"What the hell are you laughing about?" Rook asks, concerned.

"Nothing." I shake my head. "Just…I almost can't believe how quickly shit has shrapneled since we put our fingers in the fan. Two fucking weeks ago, we were going to work at our blue-collar jobs and playing fucking hockey. That's it. Now, both of you are mated, we've made forever enemies of the elites and the Council, found out our mother had the *blood of the four*, kidnapped two women, got basically kidnapped ourselves and brought here, where I'm spending my days with some of the scummiest fucking vampires on earth, in the middle of *this* fucked-up shit, balancing blending in with preparation, and all the while, trying to…*deal with* the effects of the call to my own mate." I shake my head. "It's just come apart much faster than most things do."

"That's because we're trying to keep it together," Kane says sagely. "The things you want to destroy hold together like glue."

"Yeah," I agree. "Glue formed in the minds of depraved, powerful men. They need a taste of our fucking lives for a change."

"So, what are we going to do about it?" Rook challenges. "I feel useless just sitting here waiting for you to figure it out. But we don't have access to anything electronic, and up until now, we've had exactly zero contact with the outside world."

"You don't need access," I say, not bothering with filtering as the words hit me out of the blue. I can't believe I didn't realize it before now, but we literally come equipped with the tools we need, straight from our parents' factory.

When they doubt me, drawing their brows together and sharing a look that I know all too well is to confirm I'm full of shit, I push harder.

"You *don't*. Kane can sense intention. You can read minds when you're invited in. But maybe, with my help, you don't need to be invited."

"What do you mean?" Blair asks.

Kane's voice is unbelievably soft as he explains it to her. "Cal means he can be a vessel. We don't have the access, but he does. If he opens us up to his conversations, to his interactions...we can read the people as though we're there ourselves."

I nod. "You're already stronger because of your bonds. I think there's a lot of stuff you could do if we tested your limits. You just haven't had the space or time to practice yet."

"Good. Then it'll be your job to converse with as many people as you can," Rook agrees. "Vampires, women. Everyone. Stay open to us, and we'll focus on analysis. Surely there are some ghosts hanging out in these closets that we can use."

"Though, there is one other option," I add. "And I think you should consider it."

"What?" Rook asks.

"The four of you should leave. The door's unlocked now. Escape, and leave me to handle the rest."

Kane scoffs. "Not a chance in hell, brother. We're in this together. Kidnappings, murders, auctions, and all."

I nod. I wish I could say I wouldn't do the same, but I would. For my brothers, I'd do anything.

And I can't deny it'll be a nice change of fucking pace to feel like I'm consorting with these deviant fuckers for an actual purpose.

"All right. I'll focus on Lucian too," I say. "I think there's more there, and I think we're at a real disadvantage if we don't understand it. I asked him some questions about Mom this morning, and I think there's even more to the story than we realize. More he's not saying. Maybe even more he will if I ask the right questions."

Kane glances to Rook before tiptoeing into the next subject precariously. "And the fated mate thing? How's that going?"

My chest seizes. I can't tell them the risk I took last night. They'd lose their fucking minds if they knew the extent of how much time I spent in her room—that I kissed her knowing I had no choice but to leave her behind. But I know I've got to give them something.

"I…well…we…" I pause on a sigh. "I guess we… We know her."

"We know her?" Kane's brows pull together. "What do you mean, we *know* her?"

"Romy Spencer. From Boston Prep?" I offer.

"Romy Spencer is your mate?" Rook asks incredulously.

I shrug. "Evidently, yes."

"Who's Romy Spencer?" Blair whispers to Kylie, who, trying to listen to the rest of our conversation, puts a finger to her lips.

"And how's it going?" Kane asks, his gaze searching mine intensely.

I shrug.

Rook frowns. "You did something stupid last night, didn't you?"

"Stupid, maybe. Worth it, definitely," I say, sugarcoating the full truth. "We got a chance to talk. I think she trusts me."

"Talk, huh?" Kane challenges with a smirk. "Is that all you did?"

"Shut up, Kane," I retort with a punch to his shoulder.

He guffaws. "Oh my God. I was joking. What else did you do? And more than that, *how* did you do it? Don't they have the women secluded somewhere?"

Fuck it. Our best defense is a strong offense. I have to be honest about what happened.

"She's in the room at the end of the ladies' wing. I snuck in through the window."

"Well, I'll be fucked. I didn't know you had it in you, stud." Kane winks at Blair. "It's always the quiet ones, babe. Always."

I smile, taking the jab good-naturedly. "Personality traits aren't singular. It's the being quiet that requires a certain…boldness."

Kylie laughs. "And what does Rook's grumpiness require?"

"A pretty girl like you," Kane replies, making us all laugh out loud. It's almost as if we aren't here. As if our lives are like they were before, only better.

I shake my head lightly, wishing like hell that were the truth. Rook, evidently, notices. "Ky, would you and Blair mind giving us three a minute. Maybe finish the breakfast you started?"

She nods, and Blair stands without a fight. It's not that they don't deserve to be included in every damn conversation—they're involved in the stakes. But there are demons to deal with, for myself and my brothers, and I can't in good conscience ask them to do it with an audience.

As Kylie and Blair disappear into the kitchen, I lower my voice to a murmur and lean in. "I…met our fathers."

"Fathers?" Kane asks, his voice serious.

I nod. "Unfortunately, our features have very deep biological roots. I couldn't deny their paternity if I tried."

"And there are three of them," Rook confirms. It should be a question, but it's not. It's the dot on an I and the cross of a T we wrote out a long time ago.

"Yes. Rook's father, Nathanial, is the one who selected our mother. And then he shared her with two of his brothers, Ronan, Kane's father, and Cassian…mine. And then they sold her away to be used until she died."

Rook curses, his jaw so hard I could break glass on it.

"Trust me, whatever vile picture you have of them in your heads, they're a hundred times worse." I sigh, running a hand through my hair. "But they'll pay for it. I promise. Every single sick bastard here will pay."

Instantly, Romy's face fills my mind, and everything inside me wants to rage over the mere idea of one of these vile fucks trying to claim her.

I will straight up murder before that happens.

"What exactly are you going to do?" Kane inquires, the taut line of my every muscle unmistakable.

"Where are you going?" Rook asks when the only response I have for Kane is to get up and head for the door.

"As much as I've missed you guys, I don't think we're going to dismantle the Elite Council with me hanging out here. I'm going to do my job. You guys do yours."

"Aye-aye, Captain." Kane salutes and Rook smiles.

It might not seem like it on the surface, but it's the most reassuring response I've ever gotten.

If the Slater brothers have anything to say about it, by tomorrow night, this whole fucking place will be up in flames.

And Romy will walk away alive.

13

ROMY

EAVING THE RELATIVE COMFORT OF MY ROOM for a second night of drinks and mingling has my stomach in knots I didn't even know were possible.

Overhand, bowline, square—they have *nothing* on this shit, and trust me, I know my fucking knots. My dad is a boatsman. At least, that's what he *loves* to call himself.

Every summer, he'd take my mom and me over to Provincetown, Cape Cod, to stay for a week and then sail his boat down to Martha's Vineyard. I wish I could say it was a fond memory that makes sending me to this shit feel like it's really out of character—but my dad has always been the same.

Quiet. Authoritative. Selfishly driven and spineless when it counts.

Pressing a palm against the soft burgundy fabric of tonight's velvet dress, I turn to the side to take the steps down the staircase with care. My heels are precariously tall—by my mother's decree—and my legs shake like they belong to a newborn colt.

Tonight, we won't just be with the women. Tonight, the

vampires will be joining us—and not just the one who kissed me last night. All of them.

I imagine they'll be testing us in some way. Seeing how moldable our will is and how easily we break. I wish like hell I knew if it would be safer to be accommodating or to press—but I fear the real answer is that there is no safety net here.

One way or another, at the end of the process, you leave with a vampire.

"Hey, Romy," Hillary greets, meeting up with me about halfway down the staircase. Her heels are a much more manageable three inches to my six, and I wish a little harder that I'd fought my mother on the shoe issue.

"Hey, Hillary." I force a smile, even though everything feels painfully off.

Though, she looks good. Gorgeous, even. A blue chiffon gown makes her eyes seem twice as big and bright as normal. Her lips are painted a coral pink, and her skin shimmers like she's used some sort of body balm.

I, on the other hand, am wearing minimal makeup and considered not showering, just to make myself a little less appealing.

The effort to put myself together is the very lowest I've made all day, because during the rest of the time, I've been a girl on a mission to burst some naïve bubbles.

This morning, after a quick workout and conversation with the girls I already knew during our fitness time, I encouraged both Hillary and Abigail to gather a larger group to sit with us for lunch. They did—Abigail has been quite the social butterfly since arriving and knows nearly everyone—but it didn't do me much good, seeing as I couldn't get a word in edgewise around the palpable excitement over tonight.

How handsome they would be. The things they might say. The thrill of a new crush and then being chosen by him tomorrow.

They had a dozen positive twists on something I see as the worst experience of my life, and while that hindered my progress, it also made me sad.

Sad for them. Sad for the letdown when the truth is far less pretty.

Determined to make headway, I regrouped and focused on the afternoon spa event for planting my seeds, and because of how weird it was on a basic level, I was fairly successful.

Women who showed up expecting massages and facials were met with IVs and blood-filtering machines instead. It was very Dr. Frankenstein-esque, and I could tell by the looks on several of their faces, they were wondering what the hell they'd gotten themselves into.

I can see now, though, that the time back in their rooms and the exercise of getting ready for a party tonight has renewed some of their positive energy, and it's my job now to find a way to squash it without being so much of a buzzkill they all stop talking to me.

Easy, right?

Hah.

"You look really nice, Hillary," I say finally, the words feeling out of place with everything else rattling around in my head, but very much needed to cultivate her trust.

"Thanks," she says graciously, accepting my compliment. "I tried, but I'm not exactly a dab-hand with makeup. My mom hired a makeup artist for me yesterday, who came before I left the house. All I had to do last night was a few touch-ups, so I did the best I could."

I laugh a little. "Mine did too. But not because I can't do it myself. She just knew I wouldn't if left to my own devices."

I present my face as evidence, but instead of laughing, she tilts her head thoughtfully to the side. "Why do you think you're *so* opposed to this whole thing? I mean, don't get me wrong, I understand the hesitation. I'm undecided too. But I've kind of…" She shrugs. "Been trying to get used to the idea, I guess. You don't really seem like you want to, but for me, I feel like it's the best thing I can do. I don't want to resent my life. Especially preemptively. I mean, what if it's great?"

"Yeah, I don't think this is the kind of idea I can get used to." I shake my head, trying not to drag her into the pit of despair before she has to go out there and put on a happy face. I want her to doubt—not put herself in real danger by outwardly objecting to the fucking vampires. "My mom and dad have been prepping me for this for years. So, it's not as if I haven't had time, but I don't know… I just pictured something more…romantic for myself. I don't want to settle. Why should I have to settle? Why should *any of us* have to settle?"

She nods, lowering her voice as we slow behind a group of other girls at the door to the ballroom. "Meet a guy, be courted, fall in love."

"Yes," I agree. "Exactly. This is a great group of women. The best of the freaking best, purportedly. And we're supposed to be cool with having everything picked for us instead of having any say?" I scrunch up my nose. "Seems weird."

I think about Cal scaling the building last night to climb in my window like some kind of unhinged superhero and telling me we're freaking *fated mates*.

The same Cal I used to follow around like a shadow when I was a little girl. The one I chose before I even knew what choosing meant.

It's not my choice either, but somehow, it feels different.

Irrational or not, deep down, I feel like something in me has been waiting for him all along. And the second he kissed me, something inside me...*clicked* into place.

In a weird way, it seems as if being here *is* my path to romance. As fucked up as it is. And that Cal is fated to me *because* I chose him so early on.

I can't say that to her without exposing Cal or betraying him by putting his trip to my room at a statistically higher chance of being revealed, though, so I settle for the next best option—saying nothing at all.

"I get that, Romy. I do." Her smile is soft and thoughtful—hopeful in a way that stings. "But maybe...maybe being this *adored*...this *useful*...this *powerful* for someone else, so much so that these men are basically fighting over us... Maybe it could be good too?"

Good? *Yeah, somehow, I don't think anything good for women includes the loss of free will and having to be locked and guarded in their rooms at night just to sleep,* but I don't bother explaining that. I've already said it. She already knows. She just needs time for the doubt to fester.

"Yeah. Maybe," I say instead, trying to comfort her with a small smile.

She snorts. "Wow. You really shouldn't ever play poker, okay?"

I shrug. "I'm sorry. Really."

"It's okay," she reassures with a shake of her head. "It's a wild thing, coming here to be selected by a vampire and giving up your entire life as you've known it. We're all handling it the best we can."

Okay, that clinches it. Her sweet nature is too good to ignore. The friendship with Hillary is a solid plan, and if and when I find a way out of this mess, I'm taking her with me.

"You're so right," I confirm, squeezing her hand as we take our turn through the door to the ballroom and fan out to the side where waiters are standing with trays of champagne. I grab a glass for me and a glass for Hillary, handing it to her.

She takes it gratefully, and we both down a quick sip before working our way to the side of the room where an immensely intimidating crowd of men is waiting. The sight is overwhelming, and our newly found silence only confirms it.

This shit is Scary Central on steroids.

Sharp black tuxes, strong, shapely jaws, and height so imposing it seems genetically impossible for this many guys in one room to possess it, are the most common, immediate themes. My stomach churns as they pick out women with their eyes, calling them over without taking even a step in our direction. Maybe it's the comfort of familiarity—or maybe it's something else—but I'm drawn *strongly* toward Cal.

His safety. His comfort. His protection.

If I'm supposed to be talking to one of these guys, I want it to be him.

He stands in the far back corner of the ballroom, a glass of amber liquid in his hand and a hard set in his jaw. He looks incredibly handsome—he always did, even as a kid—but he also looks angry. My system wars with the dichotomy, but my legs keep moving.

I'm halfway to him when a voice I can't quite place fills my ears, giving me a polite order. *"Please. Don't come to me first."*

When I stop cold, Cal's eyebrows lift noticeably.

"Can you hear me?" he asks, this time much more clearly. It's startling because at this distance and with the complete lack of volume—it's not like he's shouting—there's no way I should be able to hear him.

But I can.

Somehow.

I nod shakily, trying like hell not to freak out. I mean, this is weird. How in the world can I hear him talking to me from this far away? *Because of fate,* my mind whispers.

"Good. That's good," Cal tells me. "I know it's probably scary, but I need you to trust me. And if you can't do that, trust the boy you once knew, okay?"

Visions of the way Cal was when we were kids—kind, quiet, observant—do the impossible and overrun the very palpable fear of this ballroom. They take me to the playground outside school, where I cornered Cal at the top of a slide for a kiss. He'd been startled—I was three years younger than him and barely on his radar—but from that moment forward, he'd been careful with me. He spoke softly. He smiled back. He listened when I jabbered, even if he had nothing to add at all.

All the questions I have about why he'd be *here*, at this undefinable, most horrible place, and his promised forthcoming explanation fade to the background, and the instinct to trust him to protect me takes over. I don't understand it—probably because it makes no sense, given I haven't known anything about him since we were thirteen and ten respectively—but just like I told him last night, I *do* trust him.

Because it's Calloway Slater.

Because…you belong to him just as much as you've always felt he belonged to you.

"Okay," I ask almost inaudibly, hoping he'll be able to hear me too and trying not to move my lips like I'm some kind of ventriloquist. "So…who should I talk to?"

"The women," he says quickly, turning to face a different direction. To the average onlooker, we don't look like we're engaged with each other at all, and I get the sense that's the way he wants it. "If a vampire calls you over, go, but do your best to keep your answers surface-level. And do not, whatever you do, mention knowing me."

"I don't like this." It's a simple statement from an overwhelmed woman with no options but to comply. I want to complain more. To beg for an explanation or talk him into running out of this room and never looking back. But I can't.

Not here. Not now.

Maybe not ever.

"I don't like it either," he replies, and for the first time since he started our conversation, I'm really not sure if the words are meant for me or for himself.

Spinning slowly, I look for a woman to be a lifeline and find Abigail first. Her expression is hopeful as she waits for a man to pay her interest, and her bright fuchsia gown does its job by standing out.

I don't want to get noticed, but maybe if I'm hiding behind her, she'll be a buffer of sorts.

It's hard because she's so focused on the men, but eventually, I catch her eye. I move toward her, only stopping when I've put her body between me and the men. "Hey, thanks again for the extra schedule."

"No problem," Abigail says, putting her back to me and smiling at a huge man with an imposing scar over his eyebrow.

"I enjoyed chatting with you at lunch and the—"

When he smiles back at her, she lets out a little squeal and interrupts me bluntly. "Sorry. I'm being summoned."

I sigh, not bothering to say anything to her retreating form as it picks up to a jog.

The crowd of women is dwindling now, and the safety-in-numbers game is becoming more and more impossible. I try to hide behind a group of women I haven't met before, but within thirty seconds, they're all long gone.

An older man watches me intently before jerking his chin at the man standing next to him. With dark brown hair and matching eyes, he cuts a shiver straight through me at the very first meeting of our eyes.

My chest yanks, and immediately, without the directive of my own brain, I'm moving toward him. It's fucking terrifying, and my eyes skitter through the room in a panicked sweep, trying to find Cal.

"It's okay," I hear his voice say on a whisper. "I'm watching. Just remember…keep it surface-level. Don't mention me."

I dip my chin in acquiescence and extend a hand to the waiting one in front of me. However, the man standing beside him—the one who was watching me and whose green eyes are borderline neon—smacks it away before we make contact.

"No touching," he chastises him. "Remember, Nathanial?"

I startle, but as *Nathanial* smiles at me, I force my stomach to settle.

"Sorry, Lucian. You know I lose my wits around a beautiful woman sometimes."

I clear my throat around the knot that's formed there.

"I'm Lucian Wrath, dear," the older man with the green eyes introduces himself. "And this is my brother Nathanial. What can we call you?"

"R-romy," I stutter, my nerves getting the best of me. Immediately, Nathanial's eyes flutter down to my throat and linger there, but Lucian's focus never leaves my face.

"And what's your last name?"

"Spencer," I say, swallowing hard against the sudden dryness in my throat. "Romy Spencer."

"Ah, Spencer," Lucian says warmly. "That's why you look familiar. I knew your great-aunt Lucille."

My stomach tenses at the casual remark. To him, it's supposed to be comforting, I suppose. But all it does is remind me of a relationship I never had. My father's aunt was the last generation of Spencers to be selected before me, and because of that, she wasn't around to get to know me.

I try to soften the edges of the sting, but the words still come out brittle. "That's nice. I never got the chance."

"I sense a little bit of an attitude in this one, Lucian," Nathanial teases. "Would probably be quite fun to work out of her."

As if the comment isn't off-putting enough, the fact that he's talking *about* me instead of *to* me serves as a clincher. Nathanial is not the ideal vampire to end up with, that's for damn sure.

Not that there is an ideal option, but this is the kind of break-down I'm being forced into.

If Hillary or Abigail mentions him in passing, I don't think I'll be able to be chill.

"Please, dear, don't mind my brother," Lucian says, his voice filled with apology and frustration. "He's apparently misplaced his manners tonight. Why don't you ask us something about ourselves if you'd like? No question is off-limits. Give yourself a bit of ground back, perhaps?"

"Okay," I say, my whole body taking on a tremble. The invitation to ask any question in the universe is too good to pass up, even if it scares the living shit right out of me.

Oh, well. Here goes nothing…

"I guess…the thing I'd really like to know. The question that nags at me the very most is this. What, exactly, is so appealing about *buying* a woman rather than wooing one yourself? Is it an ineptitude issue? A tiny dick thing? Or are you really just that self-important?"

CAL

"So, what are your hobbies, Calloway?" a woman with a blue dress and friendly eyes asks kindly. "What do you like to do for fun?"

"Calloway is new to money," one of the vampires named David interrupts with a sneer before I can answer back. "He probably doesn't do much you'd be interested in."

After seeing Romy enter the ballroom with a woman named Hillary sporting a smile, I knew she'd be a safe bet for easy small talk. And I was right. We picked up conversation easily, and for the last two minutes, she's been doing a good job of keeping me busy.

It wasn't until one of David's friends started calling to her too that things got messy. Some prick named Miller joined, and then dickwad David, along with a woman named Whitney and three other vampires from whom I've yet to catch a name.

It's becoming obvious by their smiles that they aren't here to make friends with me.

"Good grief, these fucks," Kane confirms in my ear. "This is a planned humiliation ritual. Or it's supposed to be, if they weren't so bad at it."

Yeah, I verify to Rook. *That makes sense.*

"I suppose David is right, for the most part, Hillary," I answer without shame. "I do work a lot. But my brothers and I are fond of hockey, and I rebuilt a Camaro last year that I drive on the weekends."

"That's really cool." She smiles again, happy enough with my answer to ignore David entirely. I can tell from the flare in his fiery eyes that he doesn't like the snub one bit. "I actually grew up watching my brothers play hockey, so I certainly understand the sport."

Continuing the conversation is the natural next step, but when Romy's shaking voice cuts in to my consciousness, I can't hear anything but her. I've done my best to handle three conversations at once up until now, but at the fear in her voice, hers takes absolute precedence.

"What, exactly, is so appealing about *buying* a woman rather than wooing one yourself? Is it an ineptitude issue? A tiny dick thing? Or are you really just that self-important?"

Jesus, Romy. As soon as the words leave her mouth, I drop the conversation with Hillary and David and the others like a hot stone, dismissing myself as politely as possible.

"Excuse me for a second, Hillary…Whitney." I don't bother with the men's names. "I'm afraid I need to step away for a minute."

Hillary nods, though her smile falls a little, but I don't have time to linger on it as I move.

Between one moment and the next, I find myself across the party to the group of three—Lucian, Nathanial, and Romy—and turning it into four. Lucian's smirk tells me he's not entirely surprised by my arrival, which puts me on edge from the start.

"Well, hello, Calloway," he says, a peculiar smile curling his lip just enough to be noticeable. "What can I do for you?"

"I'm just mingling my way through the room, and this conversation looked like it'd be interesting to be a part of."

"Oh, it is," he agrees. "It is."

"Romy Spencer, meet my nephew. Calloway Slater."

"Nice to meet you," I say innocently, begging my body not to betray me. This isn't the time to imagine my lips on hers or the feel of her hair sliding through my fingers. This isn't the time to picture her gasp as I touched my tongue to hers or the way her toes curled onto the wood floor as I climbed into the window toward her.

This interaction isn't the time for any of that—*not even close.*

"Nice to meet you too," she says back, following my lead dutifully.

Fuck. I'm beyond proud of her.

It's nearly impossible to imagine how hard it must be for her to keep her composure, keep my secret, and work through the fear of trusting me all at the same time. This is an overwhelming experience for me—and I'm faster and stronger than she is by a thousand.

"Romy here was just challenging us to explain what makes the selection process superior to a traditional courting," my uncle says, undoubtedly trying to stir the pot and angering Nathanial all over again.

"We don't have to answer to you," Rook's deadbeat dad spits predictably, swinging his drink around with a meaty hand and calling more attention to the four of us than is necessary.

I call on Kane through Rook, scanning the room to give him some direction. *Read some intention of the crowd around me, if you would. Things are feeling more tense than usual, and I need to keep my listening to the current conversation.*

"Ah, yes. But wouldn't it be better if we did?" Lucian challenges with a contrarian smile. "After all, I did challenge her to ask anything she wanted, and that's what she's done." He pauses and looks at me. "Cal." The nickname feels foreign from him, so much so that it brings my brows together. "Why don't you take the honor?" he says then, catching me off guard and bringing the ball of power back into his court from this morning.

He's forcing me to be something I'm not. Forcing me to play devil's advocate by explaining this auction like it's a good thing and doing it knowing I'll put myself and Romy at risk if I don't.

I can only hope she'll see through the act enough not to lose trust in me and start believing I'm the monster I've promised I'm not behind closed doors.

"Of course." My jaw grinds as I work to find the technical explanation with no rosy embellishments. I find myself falling back on the textbook definition. "Selection is…a long-standing tradition with roots in mutual respect and benefit. Some of the women back then—though of noble blood—lived a life of struggle and servitude. Vampires, likewise, found themselves powerless to control their lives or to better their families' lives, and completely depleted of the most useful gifts and abilities. A treaty was born. Vampires would be given access to the best blood, and in exchange, these noble humans would be given the means for a better life."

"Very good, Calloway," Lucian praises, making the hair on the back of my neck stand on end. My instincts are spot-on, of course, and he pushes harder, forcing me to go further. "And in this modern setting? Have we seen a benefit?"

"In some ways," I force myself to agree. "The human families who once struggled are wealthy. The vampires who've partaken, the strongest."

"Mmhmm," he hums.

I work my jaw, willing my racing thoughts to calm. Romy's eyes are wide and scared, and the sight of it makes me feel like I'm burning alive.

"That doesn't make it the only way, though," I find myself challenging. The compulsion to bring her back to center is too strong. "Not even close." My uncle smirks, and Nathanial huffs. "But it's *tradition*." The word rolls off my tongue in its bitterest form.

A tradition that's destroyed the entire equilibrium of the vampire race, mind you. One that's born only male vampires into this world for the last few centuries—and caused the presence of female vampires to disappear almost entirely.

One that's made an entire human bloodline go extinct.

One that's brought pain and suffering and abuse and death to too many human women to count.

But yeah, *tradition*.

My uncle's smile is smarmy as he inserts his own opinion. "Romy, darling, I think you'll find the selection to be the scariest part of the process, my dear. All these vampires and so little autonomy. I understand it must be unsettling for some. But I assure you this is the very worst of it. From here forward, you'll find a height of purpose so tall you'll lose track of the ground. Adoration, gratitude, and absolute servitude from your mate. This isn't about blood in the end. But about an unbreakable bond and mutual benefit." He smiles. "Come. I'll introduce you to a few gentlemen personally. Show you it's not so bad after all."

Romy's eyes jump to me, a tell I can't blame her for at all, as Lucian puts a hand at the small of her back and guides her away.

And Lucian meets my eyes with a twist of his waist, a smirk turning up the corners of his lips. It's all the indication I need that he knows my interest in Romy exists—I only wonder if he knows to what extent.

Does he think I'm just smitten? Or does he sense the universal bond growing between us?

"Such a fucking Neanderthal." Nathanial pokes at me, fiddling with the cuff links at the ends of his sleeves. "I still can't fucking believe Lucian brought you here instead of killing you." He laughs before downing his drink. "At least he killed mine."

As he turns away on the brutally casual remark, Rook checks in. My mind has been open to his and Kane's interpretation tonight, as discussed, and right now, I'm glad to have the extra ears.

Did he just imply I'm dead? Rook asks inside my mind.

That's what it sounded like to me, I agree.

"Well, that's real fucking interesting," Kane remarks.

I agree. Interesting, indeed.

Does that mean Lucian is the only one who knows we're all here? Rook asks, mirroring my own thoughts so exactly it's as though he's in tune with my mind. *And if he is, why did he keep it a secret?*

Neither of us answers. Because neither of us knows.

Focusing on Romy without making it obvious, I move to the bar and order another bourbon. I don't intend to drink much of it, but the act of procuring it gives me something to do other than talking to other women or killing my uncle with my bare hands.

"Where are you from, Romy?" a vampire I know only by the name Julian asks, his tone both friendly and interested.

Too fucking interested.

"Um, Massachusetts," she answers. "But the west side."

"Ah, I see. Have you ever been to the Cape? Or Martha's Vineyard?"

"Many times," she says hesitantly, her voice shaking. "We vacationed there in the summer. My father loves to sail."

"Incredible," Lucian remarks, inserting himself like some kind of fucking matchmaker. "Julian owns homes in both places. I imagine you'd find a pairing with him quite comforting."

"Oh Lucian, come on now." Julian lets out a hardy-har-har chuckle like some rich prick. "A woman as beautiful as Romy here is bound to be the subject of many, many bids. I can only hope to be so lucky as to be the winning one."

And his reply is enough to set me in motion toward them, consequences be damned. My uncle already knows Romy is a weakness. What the hell's the difference?

"Easy, Tiger," Kane warns in my ear. "Lucian is *hoping* you'll approach—it's practically hemorrhaging out of him—and Julian is harmless. Interested, yes, but I sense no real evil will. He's here because he doesn't know any better, but his intention is gentle."

I pull to a stop and spin in place, meeting the eyes of a woman across the room. She startles at the contact. Just to the side of her, Nathanial and Cassian, *my* deadbeat father, watch me closely. With no other option, I call her toward me with just a nudge of my mind.

It's the wildest shit I've ever done and feels wrong on every level.

For Romy's benefit, I reach out with a statement of comfort for her ears only. "My uncle wants nothing more than for me to come running to you. I'm going to talk to someone else, just to look busy, okay?"

As I glance in her direction, she covers her mouth to shield her quiet reply. "Okay."

Every second I'm not standing next to her feels wrong. And every fucking prick in this room looking at her feels worse.

"Tonight," I tell her. "Be ready at your window. I'll come to you again."

Before I lose whatever control I have left.

I force myself to turn away from her, even as everything in me strains to cross the room, toss her over my shoulder, and remove her from this fucked-up place.

Because she's mine to protect.

There's absolutely no way I can fight it all night. I have to see her again.

15

ROMY

NERVES FIRE ALL OVER MY BODY AS I PACE THE space in front of the armoire and wait for Cal to fulfill his promise.

I considered moving it out of the way ahead of time, but the fear of an unexpected visit from my guard or the light from my room out onto the lawn stopped me. I don't want to put either of us at risk of discovery, and from what Cal said about his uncle tonight—and the way he kept glancing over for Cal's reaction as he ushered me around the room—I have a feeling we're at even higher risk than I want to know.

As such, I'll be completely ignoring that for now.

When I returned from the mixer in the ballroom tonight, the lingerie I picked yesterday was hung with care from the closet door, and a note was pinned to the front in fancy calligraphy.

> *We invite you to the most unique day of your life tomorrow. Prepare to be adored. Prepare to be pampered.*
>
> *Prepare for the bond.*

I assume it was meant to calm nerves and build excitement, but for me, it did the opposite. Tomorrow is the day of reckoning. The day when my life is over.

Unless Cal figures out some way to kidnap me or something, but oh my God, I'm getting a little worried that's not going to happen.

Pace turning more frantic, I put my ear to the wall next to the armoire and try to peek through the window. It's impossible, of course, and all I gain is a shooting pain in my shoulder from the strain.

Heaving a deep breath, I force myself across the room and into the armchair to wait. I think of the pull I felt to Cal all night in that room and wonder about what it might feel like for him. If it's stronger or the same or if he feels it in his chest like I do.

I could barely concentrate on the other vampires Lucian introduced me to—so much so, I don't even remember any of their names.

And it wasn't even that they all seemed terrible—some were kind. It was the feeling of indescribable pain at betraying Cal.

As insane as it sounds, I don't have to work to trust him; my body does it all on its own.

The sound of a *tap-tap-tap* on glass startles me from my manic thoughts and sends me careening across the room toward the armoire. This time, it moves easily, and I'm ninety percent sure it's because I'm chock-full of adrenaline.

I unlock and shove open the window to let Cal in and then close it and the shade behind him to conceal the light of the room from pouring out as soon as he clears it.

"Thank God you're here. I've been going just a little bit crazy."

He winces and smiles at the same time. It's an amazing

expression—one I've never seen before but imagine I'll be seeking from here on out. It's uniquely beautiful on his features and makes a tiny dimple divot his cheek.

"I'm sorry. I had to wait for all the other activity to die down before I made the trek. Lucian, especially, is undoubtedly paying attention."

I nod. "Oh yeah. I don't think he knows I noticed, but he was looking at you all night. Everywhere he took me, he looked for your reaction."

"He knows you mean something to me. I just don't know to what extent. If he realizes you're my mate or not."

"Your mate," I repeat.

"Yes. My fated mate."

I giggle nervously. "Right. I mean, I know you said that last night, and it's not that I didn't believe you, but it's…wild. Surreal, honestly. I guess I didn't realize that was a possibility with the way my mom and dad always talked about this whole thing. I thought you—well, we…the women—were bought, and that was that."

He frowns "They keep the information that way on purpose. It wouldn't do to have all these women believing they had fated mates out there. That would make this seem all the more unromantic."

"Yeah. Hillary—one of the girls I'm friends with—she's already teetering on the edge. One real sign that there's a vampire destined for her somewhere out in the wild and she'd be jimmying the window with me."

He smiles, but it's not happy. Not at all. "I spoke with her tonight. When I think about women like her being sold to someone like Nathanial or Lucian, I nearly lose my mind."

Nerves overrun me. I mean, I love to make jokes and light and laugh about the situation for the sake of my own comfort and shitty coping mechanisms, but this is unhinged. "Cal…I'm scared. About…everything. I mean, they left this damn lingerie hanging in the room tonight for tomorrow, and—"

He moves quickly, invading my space in less than a second. "Hey, hey. It's okay. I'm going to take care of everything. I promise."

"But how? I mean, you said yourself your uncle is watching your every move. Unless. Maybe you can sneak me out tonight? Just…take off. The two of us."

He cups my cheek tenderly. "I wish I could. You have no idea. But nothing would change that way. All of these women—Hillary included—they'd still be sold. And after that? There'd only be more. Every time an auction came around, I'd have to deal with the guilt of leaving."

I nod. I hate it, but at the same time, I'm proud. Proud to be fated to a man with this level of integrity. This level of care. This level of willingness to put himself in danger for the sake of others.

"I'm glad it's you, Cal," I whisper and mean it with every ounce of my being.

"That what's me?"

"That you're the one who's destined for me. And honestly, in a weird way, it makes sense. Why I was so drawn to you when we were kids. Why I'm still so drawn to you now." I swallow hard, admitting, "Even standing this close, I feel like I'll burn straight to the ground if I don't get closer."

"I feel the same," he whispers, his voice rough around the edges. "Like it'll kill me if we don't come together."

"Maybe…" I start, pausing when the insanity of what I'm

saying hits me. I mean, I've only just seen this man for the first time in over a decade in the last forty-eight hours. I hardly know anything about who he is or what he's capable of at all.

"Maybe what?" he pushes gently, his fingertips glossing through the fringe of my hair and tucking it behind my ear and lingering right there.

Still, I can't help myself or the things I'm feeling deep inside. The *need*. The want. The burn. I'm consumed by him. And Lord Almighty, I want him more than I've ever wanted anything.

"Maybe…maybe we should give in right now. Maybe we should…get as close as we possibly can."

His smile is slow and deliciously dangerous and controlled in a way that makes it feel anything but. "Romy," he murmurs. "Are you asking me to lose control with you?"

His gaze drops to my mouth, then back to my eyes, like he's already imagining it. "To show you exactly what this pull between us means?" His voice lowers. "To take you to that bed…and not stop?"

The nervous giggle is back, but this time, it's akin to something you'd hear from a hyena. I'm so freaking thrown off by my own audaciousness, I could throw up.

And yet?

I need him to take me up on the offer.

"I think…I think yes."

His chest vibrates with an unreleased growl as his hand tightens ever so slightly in my hair. When he leans forward to take my lips with his, I meet him halfway.

The truth is, it isn't even a question whether this is a good idea or not anymore; it's the *only* idea.

The only want. The only need.

And fate is behind the wheel.

Curling up onto my toes, I push my chest into his and wrap my arms around his shoulders. His fingertips find my hips and squeeze, and I jump into his arms without prompting.

Locking my ankles around his waist, I hold on for the ride as he moves to the bed so quickly the room blurs.

As my back meets the comforter and his hips fall into mine, I gulp for all the air that's escaped me and glance toward the door. "The guard out there. Do you think he'll hear us?"

Cal shakes his head. "I'll hear him first if he does."

"Do you all…can you all hear at, like, dog-whistle volume?"

"No." He smiles. "Just me. And you…apparently, when I'm talking to you."

"How is that possible?"

He traces my lips with his finger, studying the motion as he replies. "The bond. After we make love, it'll only get stronger. A lot of things will change after we seal it."

"Stronger?" I ask, mystified. "And a lot of things?"

"Mmhmm." He pauses for a long moment. "Not only will our connection intensify but we will be sealed together in every way we possibly can. Forever. And more than that, our bond will not only make us both stronger in a lot of ways, but it will make you live longer too."

I swallow, my mind trying to catch up with everything he's saying.

When I don't respond, he quietly asks, "Are you sure about this?" He touches my face with a gentle hand. "You seem nervous. And Romy, I do not want to do anything you're not comfortable with. It doesn't matter how badly I want you or how deeply the bond burns. I would never, ever betray your trust in that way."

I shake my head. "No, I do. I want it. I want and need you. Honestly, I feel like I'll go crazy if we don't. I just…I've never done *this* before. Sex, I mean."

"I know," he says gently. "None of the women here have. They wouldn't be eligible if they had."

"So, if we do…I'm not eligible?"

He smiles. "Another perk, for sure. But I have no intentions of letting it go that far, I assure you."

"Okay," I whisper, surprised and intrigued by this version of myself.

For as long as I can remember, I've been a fighter. A contrarian and an obstinate voice in my otherwise docile home and a driven woman forced to live in a subservient body.

I never held a job after graduating college, though I wanted to badly, because my parents didn't see the point. I never played on a team or participated in a club or slept over at friends' houses.

But I did sneak out and break rules, and I most definitely fought verbally every chance I got. It was me against everyone else—always.

But now, here with Cal, I'm feeling indescribably compliant. I want nothing more than to trust, to follow his lead, and to let him show me how good it could be to feel feminine and soft and willing.

"Romy," Cal whispers. "You are so, so beautiful."

"So are you," I agree. "I've always thought so. I've thought many times about the quiet boy with cutting blue eyes who made me feel more seen than anyone else ever did. About how he was… how he might be."

His lips find mine before pulling back on a gentle whisper. "All the things that I am are designed by the universe for you. To serve you. To comfort you. To please you. To love you. Without this satisfaction, I am nothing. Without you, I am hollow."

"Cal, please. Make love to me tonight. I don't think I'll survive without it."

"I feel the same way," he whispers against my mouth, kissing me deeply. "I'm drawn. Desperate. Incomplete."

"Yes." It's my every sensation down to the very last detail.

"I wish we had more time," he says then, his lips finding my forehead. "More time for me to *woo* you, as it were."

My smile aches as I sink my forehead into his chest. "I guess my question is what prompted your swift interference tonight?" I ask, a little embarrassed by how cavalier I was with risk. Both Lucian and Nathanial could have killed me on the spot for being so disrespectful, I have no doubt.

His hum is both conciliatory and humorous. "I'll never ask you to be something other than who you are, but you definitely threw me for a loop with that one."

"Sorry," I apologize, but I've barely completed the word before he's shaking his head.

"Don't be, Romy. You don't ever have to be sorry with me."

His gentle nature and fierce acceptance are all the confirmation I need to take the rest of the night in both hands.

Grabbing his hair, I pull his mouth down to mine, but this time, I don't go gently. It's an assault with my tongue, a beg and a plea and a million other desperations I can't name. I ask him to react, but more than that, I invite him to lead.

To show me the way. To take and give in equal measure, and to seal the connection between us in a way that'll never break.

"First," he says. "Your pleasure."

I swallow. "And then?"

"My pleasure."

"And then?"

"*Our* pleasure."

A shiver runs along my spine and settles in my hips. They lift toward him of their own accord, and my eyes widen. It's not that I didn't want to do it—but the call to my brain definitely came from outside the house.

"You just…"

He nods, a smile alighting in both his eyes and across his mouth. "Lie back, my love. I want your pussy to be my first taste."

Holy. Shit.

My first bout with sex is going to be with a vampire. *I might be in over my head.*

"Don't be nervous," Cal urges, scooting down the bed and pushing apart my knees. My whole body shakes, so it's not like my anxiety is a secret—still, I can't help but wonder if he somehow read my mind. "Everything about me is about you, remember? I'm built to read your cues. Built to put your needs above my own. I promise, you will have the best experience of your life, or I will throw myself on the sword trying."

A giggle I can't stop escapes my lungs. "You know, a couple vampires tonight couldn't help but talk about you. About your blue-collar background and how unrefined they find you to be."

Cal scowls, and I laugh. "It'll be our little secret for now, but I think you're better with words than all of them."

He grins. "Oh Romy, we're in good shape, then. Words, I'm afraid, are at the very low end of my abilities."

I laugh, but it's cut off sharply as he dives between my legs, sealing his mouth over the lace of my panties and sucking. My sleep shorts left so fast, I didn't even notice.

As the suction releases, my back contracts, and my panties disappear too, leaving my heated skin to a breeze from the central heat as it kicks on. Cal's tongue alleviates the shock quickly, licking a path up my center and swirling around my clit.

Air leaving me in a whoosh, my body bucks.

With soft, steady strokes, he works me into a frenzy in every sense of the word. My body, my mind, my hope—all of it soars so far beyond these walls it touches the moon and the stars.

I grip his hair tightly as he urges me on, but he doesn't complain at all. When I loosen my grip, he renews it by reaching up and squeezing with his hand.

As my other hand wanders, he finds it with his own and rubs mind-numbingly at my wrist. With every stroke he gives—both with his fingers and his tongue—the pound of my own pulse inside my ears grows louder.

It's then that I understand.

My pleasure.

Then *his*.

He meant my blood.

"Cal," I cry, the softness of my voice a pure stroke of necessity. I want to yell and scream and cry from the way he's making me feel. But with the guard right outside, I know I can't.

He doesn't reply—at least not with words. But with actions, his answer is loud and clear.

He wants me to jump, to fly, to free-fall into my pleasure and not look back. It's a vulnerability and a gift to see him like this—to have this from him. And with a single sweet touch of his palm, lying flat on my stomach as his tongue works its magic, I cascade.

Over the cliff and into the deep pool on the other side. My vision blurs and then blackens as my eyes clench, and my toes curl into his back. His tongue moves slowly as I come down off the high, and then, without delay, his mouth is at my wrist.

There's no pain as he sinks his teeth in—only a rising sense of renewed pleasure and an overwhelming wave of purpose.

They're not wrong about how powerful this feels. But I highly doubt it feels this way with the wrong person.

I cannot imagine that anything could feel like this ever, with anyone else at all.

16

CAL

ROMY'S BLOOD SINGS ACROSS MY TONGUE BEFORE gliding down my throat with both ease and excitement. As a loyal follower of the law, and a purist in my vampire ideals, this is the first time I've tasted the blood of a human before. Knowing it belongs to my fated mate—indescribable.

I imagine this is the magic of sharing a first time with your spouse on your wedding night for a human male—or hell, maybe it's better.

I guess I'll never know beyond my own experience, and for that, I'm actually grateful.

This moment. This bond. It's incomparable, just as destiny intended.

Cutting off the flow with a swipe of my tongue well before Romy would get dizzy or depleted, I crawl up her body until my hips fall between hers. She's breathing heavily, but her eyes are alight with pleasure.

"All right?" I ask softly, touching my lips to hers with a gentle peck.

"All right?" she repeats with a laugh. "Yeah. It was all right. Freaking hell."

I laugh, admittedly feeling a little cocky. "That good?"

"World-changing," she replies, her voice devoid of even an ounce of humor. Leaning down, I take her mouth in another kiss, this one deeper, sweeter, and longer.

"For us both," I declare as soon as the kiss breaks. "Your pleasure. My pleasure…"

"Our pleasure," she says, picking up my lead beautifully.

Pants gone in one blink of her eyes, I sink my hard cock inside her in one slow stroke. Her pussy is tight around me like a vise, and she gasps when I push through the final barrier and fill her completely.

But once every inch of my cock is fully seated inside her, I watch in fascination as her eyes fall closed in rapture.

"Cal…" she whispers, her warm breath brushing my skin. "This is…this is…"

"The best thing I've ever felt." I don't know if it's her thought or mine or a combination of both. But they are the truest words I've spoken in this lifetime.

Romy and I, together, are magic.

Kismet. Fate. Destiny.

All of it.

I get the hype. I get the yearn. I get the burn.

This…*this* is what life is about.

"Are you okay?" I ask, my voice the shakiest it's ever been. It's nothing of the strength, power, and grit vampires are known for—but its significance is so much more.

This level of openness and consideration for another is far

more impressive than a record speed, weight lifted, or ruthless-ness will ever be.

"Yes, Cal. Please," Romy begs. "Give me more. Give me all of you. I need it desperately."

Moving slowly, I stroke in and out until the needy grasp of her fingernails grows. She scratches at my back and my arms and my chest, and the keen of her wail is growing almost too loud to conceal.

I take her mouth with mine, swallowing it down, and up-ping my tempo as I do. Each drive of my hard cock makes her breasts bounce against my chest and tiny gasps of air escape from her lungs.

But then she shocks the ever-loving-shit out of me by taking my hand and placing it on her neck, forcing my fingers to feel the pounding pulse near her throat. "Do it again," she begs. "Drink my blood."

My cock jumps inside her, the excitement almost too much to contain, but also, this is Romy. My Romy. The last thing I want to do is put her at risk. "Romy, no. I can't."

"Please," she pleads, grabbing at my shoulders and pulling me even closer to her. "Just a little bit. I need to know what it feels like to have you feed off me while you're inside me."

I shut my eyes. *"Romy."*

But she places both of her hands to my cheeks and forces me to meet her desperate gaze. "I need it, Cal. I need it more than I need anything right now."

I want to deny her, but I can't fucking deny her.

Mouth to her neck, I rub my lips against her neck, and let my nose inhale the undeniably addictive scent of her blood. Her pulse thrums beneath my tongue, and I can only hold back for a good three seconds before I sink my teeth into her skin.

Her blood floods my mouth, the delicious taste of it hitting my tongue and sending a flood of pleasure through my veins.

She moans and her breaths come out in erratic pants, and I don't think my cock has ever been this hard in my entire fucking life.

I drive myself deeper and deeper, and she responds by wrapping her legs around my hips and moving her body in rhythm with mine. Her lips are parted and her eyes are hooded, and she's so fucking beautiful it makes my chest ache.

I feed and fuck and make love to her all at the same time.

I taste her blood and fill her with my cock, and I release my teeth from her skin when I can tell we're both on the precipice.

She shakes and moans, and as the pressure of pleasure's explosion builds in my spine, so does her grip on my shoulders.

Physically, I could go all night and never tire. But emotionally, I need the completion more than she needs her next breath.

I need to fill her with my come. Every cell inside my body wants to breed her, wants to fill her belly with my baby, wants to make her mine in every fucking way I can.

As she crashes over the edge again, cascading into pleasure and climax and relief, I drive my cock as far as I can go and come deep inside her, marking her, claiming her, making her mine forever.

And the bond between us seals like a closing door.

Here, like this, as one with her, I am complete.

"Romy."

"Yes?"

"I love you," I tell her, even though those words don't even come close to what I feel for her. "Body, mind, soul, fucking everything. I love you."

"I love you too," she whispers back.

"And thank you."

She quirks an eyebrow.

"For the greatest gift I've ever been given in my life."

She giggles lightly before shrugging. Her joke is soft and loving as she says, "You're welcome."

I gently tuck her hair behind her ear, touch my lips to hers, but then freeze.

My head snaps toward the door, every instinct in me shifting in an instant. There are extra footsteps in the hall, and I fear the perfect cocoon we've been living in has just fallen from the fucking tree.

"Fuck. Someone's coming," I say so quickly, it's harsh. My hands tighten on her body, unwilling to let go.

I don't move right away. Every part of me is screaming to stay, to damn the consequences and keep her exactly where she belongs. *With me.*

But I have to. "Fuck, I'm sorry. I have to go."

She nods fervently, even as her fingers clutch at me for a half second longer.

"Push the cabinet back," I order, already moving, already fucking hating it. I dress and climb onto the edge of the window with inhuman speed.

She jumps up and runs on tiptoes to follow me, stopping me for one final kiss that almost undoes me entirely.

I almost don't stop.

I almost don't leave.

But instead, I nod for her to shut the window and put my palm against the glass, mouthing, *I'll see you tomorrow.*

She nods and pulls down the shade, and with no other option, I drop directly to the grass below.

The fantasy of tonight has ended, and reality is back with a slap.

But the bond doesn't loosen.

If anything, it tightens and tugs and threatens to pull me back toward her with every step away I take.

My muscles shake and my mind frenzies as I work my way through the woods toward my brothers' villa on the far side of the property.

I knew leaving Romy after completing the bond would be bad—but I had no idea of the intensity.

Withdrawal makes my skin pebble, and my brow shines with sweat. I feel nauseated, and the pit in my gut sits heavy like lead. My movements are still sharp but notably sluggish, and my chest rages with a burning tightness the likes of which I've never felt before.

I don't regret what we did, but I'll be damned if I didn't underestimate the effect.

With one last burst after surveilling the open space between the edge of the hedgerow and their villa, I run to the door and through it, Kane having been standing at the ready as I arrived. He puts a finger to his lips in welcome and then ushers me to the living room, where Blair and Kylie are both sleeping. They look like they're out—exhausted, no doubt, from days on end of isolation, fear, and helplessness—but the last thing I want is for one of them to awaken to my brothers and me strategizing while I look like this.

I jerk my chin toward the women. "Maybe we should leave them out of this."

"Let's go in the kitchen," Kane agrees, prompting Rook to extricate himself from Kylie and follow along.

I go straight to the cabinet for a glass, fill it with water from the tap, and down it in one swig.

Kane wastes no time pointing out the unorthodox action. "Okay…so…you're drinking now? Like…a human? What the hell is going on, Cal?"

I shake my head. "I'm…feeling sick. And I thought it might help."

"Feeling sick?" Rook interjects. "We don't get sick."

I close my eyes and scrub at my face, beating him back as he tries to get inside my mind with a familiar hammer. It's a cheap bastard move, attempting to get the answers to all his questions without giving me a chance to speak for myself, but if I saw him in this condition and had his ability, I can't say I wouldn't do the same.

I look as rough as I feel and, put simply, that can be summed up in two words—like hell.

"Okay, Cal. What's going on? What the hell happened after the mixer tonight? Last time we checked in, you were talking to the Viking-looking brothers from Hanover and listening to Lucian and the Council wax poetic about tomorrow's *ceremonies*. Is it Romy? Did she not make it back to her room safely or something?"

"I…" I shake my head.

"Spit it out," Kane insists. "We can't deal with it if we don't know."

"Romy's safe. At least…as safe as this shit gets. But after we were dismissed from the mixer, and after things quieted down in all the vampire villas, I went back to Romy's room."

"You snuck in again?"

I nod. "Not only that. We…mated."

"Oh shit," Rook groans. "You completed the bond. Tonight."

I nod, rubbing at my eyes and willing them not to cross. The feeling of codependency is shattering. I can barely maintain my fucking posture, let alone function normally.

"And then you *left*?" Kane asks incredulously. "That can't be good."

"It's not," I agree. "It's very, very bad. I don't know how the fuck I'm gonna go on with my day tomorrow like nothing's happening. I'm locked up. My fucking muscles are cramping. I feel like I could pass out."

"Well, fuck, dude. What are we supposed to do? How can we help you?"

Sarcasm heightened by my very real suffering, I don't hesitate to snap back. "Oh, I don't know. We could start by figuring this shit out so we can dismantle the fucking Council, ruin the auction, free these women, set things right, and go back to living normal lives so I can be with my fucking mate. Or second option, I'm going back to Romy's fucking room, kidnapping her ass just like you fuckers did, and hightailing it out of state to live on the run."

"Right," Kane agrees, his wide eyes finding Rook's, brows waggling.

Cal, it's okay. I can feel you. I'm okay. I'm still just in my room, alone. You can relax, I promise. I'll tell you if something's wrong.

The sudden intrusion in my brain is shocking and settling at once. It's Romy, talking to me like I can talk to Rook. I don't know how it's happening, but I don't fight it. Instead, I open myself up to it more.

My brothers notice the stillness, but I hold up a hand when Kane opens his mouth to speak.

Romy, I whisper her name in mind.

Oh God, you can hear me, her voice fills my head. *Thank God. I've been feeling you freak out since the moment you left. I didn't know what to do. I knew you'd hear me if I spoke, but I heard Lucian outside my door talking to the guard. I didn't want to chance it, even at a whisper.*

Lucian? I growl, the relief I feel from the connection with her waning temporarily as my anger fires up. *That's who was in the fucking hall?*

It's okay. They talked and he left. Didn't even knock or anything. I got the idea to talk to you with thoughts, and well, I guess it worked. I really wanted it to work, so that's good.

Are you okay? I ask, knowing this is the only thing that might actually have any legs in the effort to calm me down.

Yes, she affirms. *I'm good. I promise. Better than I've ever been. I wish I were with you, but I don't know, I guess my body understands why I'm not.*

That's good. I wish like hell I could say the same.

I know, she replies. *I can feel you. It's different than if it were happening directly to me, but intense all the same. I don't know how to explain it. Your suffering is like writing on my skin.*

We're connected, I explain simply. *Bonded. It makes sense that we'd be this in tune. I just didn't expect it.*

Neither did I. Well, to be honest, I didn't expect any of this. But Cal…you need to trust me to handle myself for now. I'm scared, but I'm ready. When you were talking about the greater purpose of helping all these women tonight, something inside me clicked. It's why I'm here. Why I couldn't connect with you earlier. Why the universe sent you back to me. I always felt like I was meant for something bigger than what my parents said I was, like a career or an invention, or I don't know, something. I never pictured this, but it makes so much sense. I'll handle myself, be ready to handle the women. You just focus on the vampires.

For the first time since I left Romy's room to sneak my way over here an hour ago, my body relaxes. She's so fucking smart and brave and beautiful. I can't believe the universe promised her to me.

God, I love you, Romy. And thank you. For being so fucking great I have no choice but to succeed. I will get you out of this. I will get all of us out of this. I swear to the end of the world and back again.

It's the craziest fucking thing, but I swear I can *hear* her smile—feel it in the marrow of my bones.

I love you too, Cal. And good. Now I'm going to try to get some sleep. Unlike you, I need it.

I can even hear her fucking cute-ass giggle in my head.

When my shoulders relax and my eyes unhaze, my brothers are standing in front of me, shaking their heads.

"Mind sharing what the fuck that was?" Rook asks when my gaze meets his.

For as fucked up as I was when I came in here, I still find it somewhere inside myself to laugh. "You should recognize it well. I was doing what you do. Talking in my freaking head. Romy… she and I can…talk to each other."

"Well, I'll be damned," Kane laughs. "These bonds sure do work quickly."

Rook smiles at that. "And I suppose we can assume all is well with the way your body has stopped freaking the fuck out?"

I nod. "Well, not *well*. But tolerable. I still hate like fuck to be apart, but she's safe. She's in good spirits. She's…so fucking brave it's ridiculous. So, yeah, I'm feeling better."

"Good," Kane teases. "Because it's going to be hard to take down a vampire empire tomorrow if you suddenly need water and air and shit."

I shake my head on a snort. "It's still going to be hard. But we're going to do it anyway. And I'm ninety-nine percent sure our dear old uncle Lucian is the key."

They nod in agreement, and I sit down at the counter to get to work.

"I've got a plan," I say. "But it's going to take all six of us to make it happen."

"Lay it out there, brother," Rook says. "We're all ears."

17

I WAKE TO THE SOUND OF A KNOCK ON MY DOOR, the deep slumber of lax limbs and bite marks on my wrist and neck slowing my eyes' opening.

The knock sounds again, intensifying in both tempo and force, and I jump from the bed in a hurry as I realize this isn't the *Twilight Zone* movie or something—I'm very much waking up in Dracula's freaking mansion for the day of reckoning, aka the wholesale market for human women.

Scuttling to my bag, I grab a sweatshirt and toss it on. Pulling it firmly over my wrist and ensuring the collar hides the small puncture mark that sits low on my neck, I make a Sharpie-level mental note that I will need to figure out how to cover up Cal's marks with makeup and jewelry really well before any other attempt of human interaction today.

And then, I hightail it to the door.

"Good morning," I chirp, swinging open the door to my waiting guard with what I hope is an easy breezy attitude. "Breakfast?"

His brows draw with slight contempt since the overflowing

tray of food makes the answer to my question painfully obvious, and then he grunts out a question.

"Would you rather a treadmill or an exercise bike?"

"Excuse me?" I ask, confused. "What do you mean?"

"Fitness this morning is being held in the rooms. You can have an exercise bike or a treadmill."

"Oh." I use my supposed human naïveté as a tool. "Why are they doing it that way? Yesterday we all worked out together."

"I don't know," he says. "All I know is that you get a treadmill or a bike."

"Oh-kay. A treadmill, I guess."

"Very good. It'll be delivered within the next hour."

With that, he hands me the tray, invades my space in a manner that forces me back into the room on a scramble, and then pulls the door shut with a hand on the knob. I hear the lock turn, and my eyes jump wider.

What the hell is going on? Why don't they want us to be together?

My first instinct is to skip the food, but as my legs shake just walking it over to the table beside the chair, I rethink the idea altogether. Sharing my blood with Cal last night was magical. Truly unlike anything I've ever experienced in my entire life.

But biologically, it makes my body have to work to produce more, and with everything at stake today, I really can't afford to let myself get hungry. I'm already working on a few hours of restless sleep.

Starting with a carb, I grab a waffle and shove it into my mouth a bite at a time without even bothering with the syrup. I'd rather do sugars in the form of fruits.

Popping one strawberry slice into my mouth and then another, I sit down in the chair and curl my legs into my chest.

The bed is rumpled from the night spent with Cal, and just the sight of it takes me right back to the feeling.

Testing the waters, I reach out to Cal through my mind again, wondering if he'll be able to hear me while he's not in as much distress as he was last night.

So, uh…is this thing still on?

I swear I can hear his grin, and it sends a thrill through me. *Hi, sweetheart. Did you sleep well?*

Not exactly well, but it'll do the job. What are you…what are you doing right now?

On my way to meet with my uncle. I've been called to a private meeting.

I frown. *Is that…is that bad, you think?*

I think it's just another mind game. He's got motives that run well beyond the ones in plain sight. But you don't need to worry. I'll be fine. In fact, this is helpful—might even aid in my plans.

Okay. I'm just…eating breakfast. My stomach is anxious, but I figured I'd better eat.

Yes. Please. I need you strong and healthy today. But this is almost over. I promise. And then you can ignore breakfast as long as you like.

I smile. *I don't think I'll mind eating if you're the one feeding me.*

And I will, Romy. My purpose from here until eternity is to lavish you with care and affection and respect and love and pretty much anything you ever want or need me to do. And fuck me, sweetheart, I'm thankful for the privilege.

I blush. *Okay, sweet talker. Focus on the meeting with your uncle and flirt with me later.*

You got it. I'll try not to think about how fucking delicious your pussy tasted last night too much.

Cal!

His laughter fills my head. *Don't worry, Romy. Go about your day with as little anxiety as you can. I'll take care of everything.*

Goodness, talk about a green-flag man. Well, *vampire*-man.

Cal, whatever the opposite of weaponized incompetence is, I'm pretty sure you have it.

Eat, love. Goodbye for now. I'll reach out when I can, but if you need me, you know I'm here.

Okay. Bye. Nerves dance in my stomach over words that shouldn't come this easily. Still, I say them. I want to. And Romy Spencer is not a coward. *I love you.*

Oh, you have no idea how much I fucking love you, Romy. But you will. It's my goal that, for the rest of our fucking lives, you will.

18

C AL

"CALLOWAY," MY UNCLE GREETS, OPENING THE DOOR with what's becoming a signature smirk as soon as my communication with Romy comes to a close.

Honestly, it's giving a certain feeling of timing that's beyond coincidental, but it doesn't matter. I need this meeting just as much as he does. I need the time, information—I need my uncle keeping me around until tonight.

"Come in." He gestures with his hand. "Or would you rather continue lingering out here in the hall for a while longer?"

Ignoring the prod, I step inside the office and wave off the lingering cigar smoke. The source is still between his fingers, and as he closes the door behind me and offers me a seat in the leather high-back chair across from his, he takes another puff.

"Would you like to smoke?" he asks.

"No, thank you." I shake my head, taking the offered seat, crossing my heel across my knee, and steepling my fingers together instead. "I'm not much for cigars at nine a.m."

He chuckles, reclaiming the seat across from me that's closest to the fireplace. There's a bar set with amber liquid on a cart along the wall, a book, open and overturned on the table beside him to keep his place, and pictures from all over the world of him and his consorts.

He looks at home here—in this office, and now that I think of it, all over the grounds—more so than any of the other vampires, and it makes me wonder if this place isn't just owned by the Council, but him.

"I find cigars enjoyable at all hours, myself," he muses. "After all, what is morning to a vampire? The sun never sets on our day."

I shrug, conceding the point. It's fucking bullshit small talk, and frankly, it's taking everything in me to sit through it. But logically, he's right. Humans follow the sun like a clock, but to us, all the hours are the same.

I make the first move, claiming the upper hand right out of the gate and addressing some long-weighing questions from my mind. "Speaking of vampires, Uncle, I find the group here interesting for many, many reasons. One of which is the way not one of them besides you seems pleased or accepting of my presence. Why is that? The Council itself has barely paid me any mind, and your brothers would much rather see me dead."

He smiles, pleased with himself and his answer as he delivers it. "They didn't want you here. Frankly, they don't. But I've earned my place, and my judgment is trusted."

"Okay, then," I hedge. "Why do *you* want me here?"

"Before your arrival?" he clarifies. "I wanted you here because it's what's right. They don't have to like you for you to be of the fourth order of blood, Calloway. You deserve proper placement. The species deserves the continuation of the fourth line."

"Even if I don't want it."

"Even then," he agrees. "Sometimes, for the good of the whole, sacrifices must be made by the parts. You are where you're supposed to be."

"Why me? Why not Rook or Kane?"

He scoffs audibly, my question laughable. "Because they're already mated, of course." But ridiculous or not, I needed to ask it to set up my next move.

"Okay. Then why does Nathanial think Rook is dead?"

He pauses, pursing his lips before regaining a smile. "A bargaining chip. With my opposition on the Council. They wanted blood for your crimes, and I wanted you. Telling them Rook and Kane were dead was simply a means to an end."

"That's why you took me to my brothers, then? So, I would know they weren't?"

He shakes his head, toying with his own fingers, and it's a not-so-subtle sign that he's done answering my unfettered questions. The rest of the conversation, it seems, will be at his discretion.

Satisfied anyway, I push back in my seat, placing both feet flat on the floor, and moving the conversation forward once again. "All right. Fine. What can I do for you, Lucian? I assume there's a reason you've called me here this morning, away from the rest of the group."

He smiles, sitting back in his seat and resting his elbows on the exquisitely arched sides of the chair. "I asked you here this morning to, perhaps, settle some of your nerves about tonight. I know you're not keen on how things work here, but I still find that bringing you here has a purpose."

I open my mouth to tell him he can shove his purpose up his ass, but he holds up a hand.

"Ah, ah, now, let's keep this civil, Calloway. I didn't bring you here, to this meeting, for a fight. I brought you here to relate to you. To tell you of my first Selection and the way I viewed it. I think you'd be surprised to know how similar we are, really. How many of your thoughts were thoughts of my own."

"Sorry, but I find that pretty fucking hard to believe," I answer with a shake of my head. "Because if you had the thoughts I have right now, there's no fucking chance in heaven, hell, or the confines of Earth that you'd be here today. That this fucking auction would be taking place at all."

He smiles, sadness down-turning the corners of his eyes. "I admire your passion, I do. I see a picture that you couldn't possibly see, and for that reason, I imagine we'll never come to a true common ground." He sighs. "Did you know that your mother's first Selection was my first as well?"

I don't reply, but I don't need to—he can tell him mentioning my mother—mine, Rook, and Kane's mother—is a surprise without my having to say a word.

He laughs gently and without humor. "I am the eldest of the Wrath brothers, as I'm sure you've figured out, but I was also the last to attend Selection. I deferred for many years to pursue other ventures in education and philanthropy. I even spent a couple of years abroad. But while my father gave me a length in reins for quite a while, eventually, he tired. He didn't like the complaints of the Council. He was afraid we'd lose our station in nobility, even. I was called back with no uncertain expectations—attend the selection and choose a mate."

A woeful expression crosses his face.

"So, I did," he continues. "Helenna was declared mine in the second round of bids. And we had a wonderful life together until last year. She passed on with blood cancer." His smile is bitter. "It seems, the very qualities of her blood that made me one of the most gifted vampires of our region are the ones that made the cancer strong as well."

My eyes are sharp but my mind is sharper as I mentally ask Kane and Rook to listen for anything I might be missing in this little story. It seems relatable—sad, even. But I know there's a greater purpose here, and more than that, I know there's some kind of information we can use to our advantage.

If my uncle didn't want this life, he didn't have to have it. I'll die on that hill—quite literally, if I have to.

"I know you think you'd do differently than I," he goes on. "That'd you'd push back harder. And maybe you would. From what I've learned of you here, you're a man of many strengths."

He picks up a frame from his side table and turns it around to face me.

It's a picture of him, Nathanial, Cassian, and Ronan as kids. It's easy to recognize them—they look just like we Slaters did at the same age.

"But I want you to ask yourself what you might do if you didn't have brothers like yours—but instead, brothers like mine. What you would do if your good conscience and pure intention weren't a group project, but a solo venture? What would it be like to be a man on an island with no means of escape?" He hums, taking another puff of his cigar. "I want you to think on that. And then tell me what you would do then."

"If I were you?" I press. "I'd use that chest-crushing shit you used on me and vaporize every last motherfucker."

He laughs, and I swear, the way I can't understand him makes me feel like I'm in another dimension. He's evil. I've seen it with my own eyes. But it's as if he's playing at being a savior for the fun of it.

"Fair point well made, nephew. Though, as I'm sure you may soon understand, a vampire is only at their full power after the bonding with their mate is complete. In my youth, I was much, much weaker. I wish I could have done many things differently, but for all our eccentricities and powers in this world, there is no going back in time."

He snuffs out his cigar in the ashtray on the console table at his side and leans forward onto his knees. From this angle, he almost looks like something other than he is—an evil manipulator with the good sense to play the violin of my emotions.

"Tonight, Calloway," he says. "Tonight will erase many decades of guilt and frustration and shine a lightbulb on the reason I've brought you here. On the reason for all of it, for everyone involved. I know you'll rise to the occasion. I know you'll set your fears and your notions aside, and you'll do the right thing."

The right thing. Internally, I scoff. His *right thing* can kiss my ass.

Because I will never, *ever* come to heel.

19

AKEUP BAG IN HAND, COVER-UP JOB COMplete on my wrist and neck, heels dangling from my fingertips, and the lingerie I'm to wear on parade draped over my arm, I make my way down the stairs of this giant, moody mansion for the final time.

As instructed, my bags are packed and waiting in my room, ready for transport to the destination of my vampire's choosing when the bonding is complete, and everything I might need for the next twelve hours is in hand.

My lips tremble slightly, and my legs shake even in the ballet flats I somehow snuck past my mother and into my bag, but inside, I'm feeling remarkably calm.

Because my whole being feels complete in ways I can't describe, and because of the bond or love or…I don't know, something else that's far more intense and undefinable with words…I trust Cal with my entire being.

My life. My future. My safety. It's all in his hands, and surprisingly, that's reassuring.

When he says he's going to get us out of this before I'm in

the back of a dark van on my way to Blood Island with some dude named Vlad, I believe him.

For my sanity, at least, I have to.

"Hey, Romy," Hillary says, catching up to me on a jog halfway down the stairs. She looks beautiful, of course, and because of the change in schedule that kept us locked away in our rooms all morning, I haven't had a chance to talk to her since last night.

"Hey, Hillary," I greet. "You excited?"

Her chin jerks back into her chest, and her eyes widen just slightly as she considers me in between watching her step. "You seem…weird."

"What do you mean?"

She laughs, but it's not the funny kind. "Are you kidding? With all your humdrum stuff for the past two days, I thought you'd be *freaking* out."

I shrug. "I thought I would be too. But I don't know. Maybe it's just that I'm out of time or something, so I might as well go with it."

When she guffaws, I turn to look at her. She does look more nervous than usual, her cheeks flushed rosy-red like she's been hanging out in a sauna for a little while.

"Why?" I ask her, my voice soft. "Are *you* freaking out now?"

"Uh, *yeah*," she hisses. "This getup I'm supposed to wear seems five times smaller than when I picked it out, and I'm supposed to be *sold* to a vampire tonight. Then they locked us in our rooms all morning and afternoon, and I haven't seen the sun in two days. Of course, I'm freaking out!"

Rearranging all the shit I'm carrying to my right side, I put my left arm around her and pull her toward me in a half hug. Her body quivers against mine.

I know it's messed up, but it's the best thing I've felt in a while. Hillary being scared is normal. Hillary being scared means it's going to be a hell of a lot easier to convince her to run whenever Cal gives me the sign. Her being scared means she's probably not the only one, and the more of these women who catch wind of reality before shit hits the fan, the better.

My parents never let me do team sports, but tonight, I see myself acting as a captain of sorts.

"You just stick with me, okay?" I squeeze her shoulder once more. "We'll take care of each other. We still have a few hours to hang out and get ready, and we'll do some relaxation techniques."

She scrunches up her nose. "You know relaxation techniques?"

"Oh yeah," I lie. "Tons of them."

"Okay." She lets out a deep breath. "Relaxation sounds like a good plan."

"You bet. We'll even rope some of the other girls in if they're not too preoccupied with all the beauty stuff," I say, offering a reassuring smile.

She smiles back, but it doesn't quite meet her eyes. "Sounds like a plan, Romy."

"By the way…the guy I was telling you about two nights ago?" I ask, hoping a little bit of gossip will bring her some comfort too. Still, there are ears everywhere, so I'm cautious not to say his name aloud or to give any other details about knowing him.

Hillary glances to both sides with just her eyes. "Yeah?"

"Well, I think you talked to him last night. Just picture the nicest guy you spoke with…brown hair, blue eyes."

"Oh my God! *Him?*"

I nod. I can see the appreciation dancing through her eyes, but I don't blame her. I can't blame her. I had the whole thing last night—the real Calloway Slater deal—and he deserves every ounce of fantasy he gets.

The reality is that *much* better.

"Yes!" I agree excitedly. "He's always been dreamy. Quiet. Kind. Steady. Even when we were kids."

"Do you think he's going to bid on you tonight?" she asks then, piecing together a puzzle. It's not exactly the right puzzle, but it's close, and with the amount of information she has, it's impressive. "Is that why you're so calm?"

"Is there someone you have your eye on?" I ask instead of answering, letting her go through the ballroom door first and then following.

The large space is filled with mirrors and vanities, and women cheer and fight for spots with the best lighting ahead of us. It's all civil, but nerves are firing all over the place in the background of their excitement, I can tell.

"I…well, no." Hillary shrugs. "I don't even want to say a name. Because I did think a couple of the men were nice and very cute, but I don't want to set myself up for disappointment if it's not one of them in the end."

I nod. "That's smart."

It won't be necessary when Cal somehow puts a stop to every-thing, but it's smart, nonetheless.

"Come on. Let's go over on the far side. I see a couple of vanities together," I suggest. "I can help you with your makeup."

"Okay," she agrees. "That would be great."

I wave for her to follow me and hustle to the far side of the room for the remaining two seats together. They're in a little bit of a shadow from the chandelier, but I'm not concerned with the lighting.

As Hillary gets settled in her spot and I unpack my cos-metic bag, I do a little mental reach-out toward Cal. I know he's going to be super busy today—and that, ideally, I should dis-tract him as little as possible, but given that I haven't talked to him since he left the meeting with his uncle, I'm feeling a little antsy for contact and connection.

You free for a minute?

His voice is in my mind in an instant. *Always free for you, Romy. Always. Some times may be more ideal than others on occa-sion, but never unavailable.*

I smother a smile and a laugh, knowing if I start cackling for no reason, Hillary will become concerned. *Right. Good to know. We just got down to the ballroom to get ready, and I guess I'm just missing you.*

And maybe a little nervous?

No. I mean, yes. But not really. I'm feeling really confident in your ability to, like, knight in shining armor this whole thing, I guess.

Good. Because I have a plan, sweetheart. It may take longer than you'd like, and you may very well have to go onstage for the bid. But I promise, you won't be going home with anyone but me. And none of these women will be going home with any of these men either.

I appreciate his confidence, but…I can't deny one thing has my nerves taking a nosedive. *I'm going to have to go onstage?*

Trust me, Romy, I fucking hate it too, but it's the way it has to be. Now, I need you to listen really carefully, okay? Because I need you to follow these instructions like your life depends on it.

Okay, I respond and shut my eyes for a brief moment so I can fully focus on his next words.

If anything gets scary, you gather the women and get them outside. Cal's voice is direct and matter-of-fact as it fills my head. *Go south, to the far tree line. There's a road two miles through the woods, and a bright light that shines from the streetlamp. Follow that light, no matter what. It's easy to get turned around in the woods if you don't have a guide point.*

Okay, Cal. I got it, I say, though neither of us can deny my mood is much more hesitant.

Two other women will find you—Kylie and Blair, he adds. *They're my brothers' mates. They will help bring you to me in a safe place.*

Cal?

Yeah, baby?

I can't deny I'm getting a little scared now.

Don't be, my love. You are so incredibly brave. You've been stronger than I ever thought possible. And soon, all of this will be over.

Soon all of this will be over.

I take his words to heart and repeat them in my mind several times over.

But when I steal a glance at Hillary, I don't miss the way her lips tremble as she applies a fresh coat of lipstick.

And I push down my fear and focus on making damn sure I get her—and all of the other women—out of this god-awful fucked-up place before they become someone's property.

20

CAL

AFTER A MENTAL CHECK-IN WITH ROMY, I LEAVE my villa.

I'm freshly shaved and my tux is pressed, and unfortunately for me, Nathanial, Cassian, and Ronan are waiting for me.

They linger ominously at the end of the path from my front door, standing there like they think they're something to be feared.

But I don't slow my steps. Shoulders loose, back straight, and eyes forward, I walk straight in their direction.

They picked a hell of a time to try for intimidation—when the whole damn thing is only hours from destruction.

"Hey!" Nathanial calls as I push through them and continue on without so much as acknowledging their presence.

Truthfully, I plan to continue ignoring them, but my brother Kane suggests otherwise.

"They want to rattle your cage, but they haven't thought it through thoroughly enough." His voice fills my ears. "Engage with them for a minute—I think they'll end up giving us information."

Kane, who's swiftly taken to the new level of his powers,

has really started to perfect the art of doing ride-along intention checks for me. I don't even have to ask him and Rook to listen in at this point—they just always are. If he says it's in my best interest to entertain a conversation with our sperm donors, I believe him. Even if I'd rather eat fucking rocks.

Spinning slowly from the path ahead of them, I reply. "Yeah?"

"We just thought we'd give you a little familial advice for tonight," Ronan says. "Seeing as the three of us have been through more Selections than you'll ever dream of."

I nearly scoff. *No doubt about that.*

"What he's trying to say is that you shouldn't get your hopes up that you'll get the one you want this time," Cassian, my piece-of-shit father, adds with a smirk that sets a dimple in his cheek.

Instantly, I consider radical facial reconstruction.

"Yeah," Nathanial taunts. "The mouthy redhead you like so much, especially. I've been thinking about it a lot, and I haven't had a challenge in a while. I've decided to put in the work to bleed that attitude right out of her."

Easy, Rook warns, the rage I feel penetrating his brain from my own.

I know they're trying to egg me on, but talking about *my* mate like she's some vial to be drained is grounds for fucking war. Maybe I don't need to wait. Maybe I can—

Easy, Rook repeats. *Keep your focus.*

There's a part of me that hates how fucking right my eldest brother is, but the fact remains—he's right.

On a beat, I school my features and meet Nathanial's eyes.

"Bid on who you like," I say, offering a shrug. "I'll do the same. We'll see who wins."

Nathanial's smile falls at my nonreaction, anger reddening his cheeks instead.

And I don't stick around to see or hear any more—both for them and for me. This is a powerful place to leave the interaction, but the truth is, any more restraint required of me might just make me combust.

"Good job, dude." Kane's praise bounces inside my ears. "So fucking proud of your ability not to make that stupid fuck eat his teeth."

I growl. *You guys just be ready. Like we discussed, I think it's going to be easiest for Romy, Blair, and Kylie to control the women as they're coming offstage from the bid. They're ready with what they need?*

"Yes," Kane confirms. "They'll be waiting to usher the girls out of there and to a secure location as though they're taking them to their bonding villas. Rook and I will be waiting to back you up when the guys start to realize they're missing."

And where are you staging? I mentally question.

Just outside the observation room you'll be in, Rook answers. *Kane and I did some recon yesterday after everyone retreated to their villas. There is a supply and linen closet right across the hall.*

All right, boys, I reply, fixing my sleeves, and entering through the garden entrance of the mansion to be escorted upstairs. *It's almost showtime.*

21

ROMY

"YOU LOOK GOOD. DAMN GOOD," HILLARY ENCOURages as I stand in front of one of the full-length mirrors with hair and makeup to the nines—that she convinced me to do in anticipation of a night with Cal—six-inch heels my mother insisted on, and the skimpiest piece of fabric I've ever considered using for clothing.

All the calm I felt before is gone, and seeing myself like this, I can't imagine it's got any chance of coming back.

My stomach flips, and my legs start to shake as I spin around and head back to my makeup chair, unable to look at myself in this condition anymore. It'd be one thing if I were getting all dolled up to surprise Cal in my bedroom or something, but the idea of parading my ass in front of a hundred vampires in the next ten minutes while they compete to win me brings on a whole different vibe entirely.

I look down at my number—*yes, my freaking lot number just like some head of cattle*—and force the threat of puke back down my throat.

Ten.

A number that means in no uncertain terms that I'll be among the first group to take the stage. Hillary is sporting fifty-seven, and if they hadn't assigned them to us twenty minutes ago with very explicit instructions that we're not to switch, I'd be begging her to do just that.

"Ladies!" one of the ogres yells from the far side of the room. "This is your five-minute warning! Group one will be lining up in five minutes!"

A ripple of cheers, excitement, and a world-class heavy sigh from me fill the room with an increase in noise and pressure.

Hillary puts a hand to my shoulder and shakes, noticing how wigged out I'm getting. "Hey, it's good to be early! That means you can go out there and get the hard part over with. I'm going to be sitting back here waiting for my turn and wondering if all the good vampires have already made their bid."

I worry my lip but, at her clear need for something positive from me, do my best to rally. "Don't think like that. I know they said the men only get one bid in this round, but that means they'll be careful. Considerate. It's why we had the mixer last night, so they'd have more than just us in lingerie to go on."

I nearly laugh, the idea of me trying to calm a woman's nerves about her upcoming sale is so fucking ridiculous.

But I need her on my side. I need her willing to listen to me, so that when I have to get her and everyone else to safety to the south like Cal said, she'll go. I need her to help me convince the others, and I really, really just need a friend.

This is, without a doubt, the most intense thing I've ever been through in my life, and I've never had a girlfriend like Hillary to count on before now. Since my parents sheltered me so much, all the girls at school learned not to bother.

Spinning in my chair, I pull Hillary down into hers and grab her hands with mine, looking her deep in the eyes. "Anything that happens today, we're going to get through it. We're going to come out stronger and better on the other side, and no matter how I have to make it happen, I'm going to make sure we keep in touch. You've been a great confidante and friend to me here. I hope you feel the same about me."

"Of course, I do," she agrees easily. "We'll be friends for life."

I nod, considering what else I might be able to say to ready her for what's about to come, but the moment is cut short expeditiously.

"Ladies! The time to line up is now! I need numbers one through ten immediately!"

"Give 'em hell," Hillary says with a smile and one last squeeze of her hands.

I nod and stand, running to line up when the ogre's impatience grows. "Come, come. Hurry, ladies!"

Abigail is two spots ahead of me, labeled with the number eight, and she bounces on her toes with excitement.

I take a deep breath as the door at the front of the line opens and they start escorting us in, closing my eyes and reaching out to Cal one last time.

Here goes nothing. I'm on my way in.

I'm waiting, my love. Be confident. Be ready. Remember what I told you earlier, and I'll handle the rest, okay?

Okay, I agree. I love you, Cal.

And I, you, Romy. To the ends of the earth and back again.

22

CAL

WOMAN AFTER WOMAN IN SKIMPY UN-dergarments is brought through a door at the back of the room and helped up onto a raised platform in the center with white numbers in front of them like lots in an estate sale. Some smile and strut, while others do their best to maintain their composure under the bright, blinding lights and confusion.

I sit on the other side of a one-way mirror along with one hundred other vampires waiting to place a bid on the woman of their choosing via an iPad system intended to maintain both fairness and order among us.

My skin crawls with discomfort and disgust because this is what these men think is normal—but the real match strikes when *she* completes the line, stepping up to the left side of the platform and squinting into the light.

Auburn hair, black lingerie, and sweet cerulean eyes complete a look built with illicit intentions and blatant disregard for her fear, and a silent scream begs for freedom from my throat as I notice her tremble.

My uncle gets up with a wave and moves away, leaving his iPad behind in the seat he's just vacated. I watch him retreat for a moment, but with my mate onstage, scared for her life while a room full of evil, dangerous men look on around me, I can't prioritize him for long.

Romy squints into the glaring lights and fists her hands at her sides as her discomfort grows.

I scan the room and watch as men pick up their iPads, clicking through the screens to make their silent bids. Nathanial, the shit-stirrer, finds my eyes from his spot in front of me and winks.

I don't have to guess what it means—he's bidding on Romy, just to spite me.

What he doesn't understand, though, is that I don't respect the rules of this sanction any more than I respect him and the other men here. It doesn't matter if I have the winning bid or not—I'll kill if I have to.

I assume you're ready? I ask Rook, chambering my anger into preparedness.

Of course. Blair and Kylie are too. As soon as the bid is over, we'll make our moves.

Scanning the room again and forcing my eyes away from Romy temporarily, I spot my uncle in the back, discussing something with his assistant and Narris, the president of the Council.

I should be able to hear what they're saying, but I can't, and the temporary loss of ability is unsettling.

I look back at Romy as Lucian, Narris, and Lucian's assistant part ways, to find that she's calmed considerably. She doesn't shake anymore, and despite the bullshit reason for seeing her like this, she looks exceptionally beautiful.

"Stop!" The sound of my uncle's voice jolts my attention back to him as he takes a spot in the front of the group, unexpectedly obstructing the view of the women through the glass.

There's a titter of confusion and then quiet, as he clasps his hands in front of himself and looks down toward the carpet with a shake of his head.

When he looks back up, he's staring right at me.

"Something's happening with Lucian," Kane warns suddenly. "Intention is muddy to say the least, though."

Oh, I know, I mentally respond. *He's just stepped to the front of the room.*

"Gentlemen, I'm sorry, but I have to interrupt," Lucian commands the room. "The auction cannot go on without addressing the news I've received about a violator in our midst."

Noise ticks up again, and my uncle holds up a hand, sweeping the room with sharp, angry eyes.

"A vampire, last night, violated the isolation order and entered the room of one of the auctioned," he states through a tense jaw. "Not only that, he mated her, drank of her blood, and betrayed the treaty we hold so dear by robbing her birthright."

A wave of anger rolls through the room, men jumping to their feet all around me and demanding an answer.

"Who?"

"We'll kill him!"

Rook, I prompt, standing up and steeling my nerves. *I hope you guys are ready. It's happening now.*

"Oh, we're ready, buddy," Kane answers for him. "When the shit hits, we'll be at your back."

One of you get Romy.

"We'll take care of it, bro. We promise."

My uncle's voice is booming. "The man at large—the man you want to kill—I'm sad to admit…is my nephew. Calloway Slater."

A hundred sets of eyes meet mine, and before even a beat, the first of them is on me. I move faster, the drive of knowing Romy is just on the other side of the glass pushing me well beyond my normal limitations.

I'm faster. Stronger. Smarter. I anticipate moves before they happen and before even a moment has passed, ten men are on the floor, dead at my feet.

Two men exit immediately, running for the women, and a scream rends the air from the other room. I want to look—to check on my mate—but I know better than to spare the time. It'll get me killed.

I move with precision and ease, working my way through the room with fast hands and an even faster knife. When Kane flips a man over in front of me and breaks his neck, I exhale.

Backup has arrived, thank God.

Rook doesn't hold back, unleashing every ounce of his anger and strength on two vamps at the same time—quite literally smashing their heads together and managing to choke them to death simultaneously.

The room is fucking chaos. It's bloody and violent and as vicious as anything I've ever seen.

And as the bodies pile up, the cowards make themselves known. They don't challenge us—they hide.

The Wrath brothers are some of the worst offenders, along

with the Council members. They don't do the dirty work. They simply reap the rewards.

"The Wraths and the Council," I call to Rook, who's just felled another at his feet. "Make sure they don't leave. Without them, all of this is for nothing."

He nods, moving swiftly as Kane and I face our next challenge of vampires. They're fast, but we're faster, and the result is a bloody trip to join the other men on the floor.

Julian, the vampire who was kind to Romy, is left in their wake, but his eyes are surprisingly wide. As I approach, Kane yells to me from behind the next row of chairs.

"He has remorse! He doesn't want this!"

With no time for long-winded negotiations, I issue my own ultimatum. "Julian, help us or die. Your choice."

Without hesitation, Julian turns and stops the next approaching vampire in his tracks, sending him careening into the wall before smashing his skull against a metal table with a sickening thud.

It's all the evidence I need to continue—and to let him do the same.

This fight is far from over, but I'm too deep into it to lose.

The only option left is maximum damage.

23

FROM NERVES AND SILENCE TO UNEASE AND UN-
certainty, the moment the tempo of our debut to
the stage shifts, it's impossible to miss. This isn't
the normal process, or at least, the crew working this room and
standing guard at the door aren't acting like it as they scramble
and shout into the microphone radios at their chests.

An intense roar has built behind the mirrored wall in front
of us, and the sounds of thuds and yells and grunts soon follow.

Girls glance between one another as one of the guards steps
forward and holds a hand for us to stay.

"What's going on?" Abigail asks, all her normal bravado re-
duced to nothing. At the sound of chaos and pure brutality on
the other side, fear has finally reared its head.

"I don't know," I offer, trying to be a voice of calm. "But we
should probably go back to the ballroom."

Women scream and scatter everywhere as one of the vampires comes crashing through the mirror in front of the platform
stage they've constructed for us to parade on and lands splayed
and lifeless on the carpet in front of us.

"Oh my God!" Abigail's shriek is high-pitched and pointed as she jumps off the back of the stage.

The whole room behind the glass reveals an all-out war between the vampires, Cal at the center of it.

But before I can fully process it, a hand clamps around my arm and yanks me backward.

A strangled gasp tears from my throat as cold fingers dig into my skin, and I look up to find a huge vampire with eyes as dark as night staring down at me.

"You're coming with me, you little cunt." His smile is pure evil and a growl escapes his throat, but that growl quickly shifts to strangled grasp when two hands wrap around his throat.

"I will fucking kill you," Cal spits, his hands gripping the vampire's neck so tightly the whites of his eyes turn black.

The vampire is taller than him, but he's clearly stronger, and in the blink of an eye, Cal squeezes his throat so hard that the big bastard's body goes limp. A harsh snap fills my ears, and the vampire hits the floor with a thud.

But when another vampire lunges for Cal, he doesn't make it three steps before he just drops mid-step. His body turns to a crumpled heap of bones in a flash.

Between one heartbeat and the next, Cal pulls me to him, pressing my body tight against his chest. He kisses me, and when his eyes lock with mine for a half second, they're fierce and focused and alive.

"Go," he commands just before four more vampires start to circle him. "Go, Romy!"

I want to stay with him, I want to make sure he's okay, I want to do a million and one things, but when Cal's voice is in my head, urging me to get out, I know what I have to do.

Right now, just standing here, I'm a distraction. I'm another thing for him to worry about. And as I told him last night, those are both things I refuse to be.

He has a job, and I do too.

And it's about damn time I start doing it.

I jump down from the stage, sprinting over to where the rest of the women are panicked on the far side of the room. "Hey! Everyone! Follow me!" I raise my voice over the din and start herding them, unstopped by the guards now that they've scattered to join the fray. "Come with me!"

Panicked enough to listen, they follow my direction in droves until we're out in the hallway and looking for a place to get away from the danger. The other women are here too, having heard the commotion from the holding room set up in the ballroom, and as we all run around in our lingerie, it makes the weirdest scene of scattered ants I've ever seen.

It's like a bomb threat at a strip club, for Pete's sake.

"Hey!" I yell on another command. "Everybody listen to me so I can get you to safety!"

The women are wide-eyed and terrified, and a quiet hush falls over the group as they point me out to one another and huddle together. Suddenly, the pressure to come up with an escape plan feels monumental. Cal was explicit with the instructions of where I was to go, but as expected, he didn't provide much insight on how to convince the women to come with me.

"As you can see, things are turning bad," I say, the understatement of the century a trademark of my discombobulation that'll go down in history. "I know what to do, though, so I need you all to remain as calm as possible and follow me."

"Come on!" Hillary shouts, stepping up to the plate as my VP of Operations. I'm so freaking thankful, I could cry, but I don't. The tears will only blur my vision, and I'm going to need that to escape. "Follow Romy!"

Hustling quickly, I usher them back down the hall and past the steps we've taken to our rooms every night with only hopes and freaking prayers that there's an exit in this direction. I'm going on nothing more than instinct and lack of choices, as all the violent chaos and commotion from the men is currently doing a great job of blocking every other direction.

I glance over my shoulder, looking back as we run in a group of flying hair and wispy undergarments that would do the Playboy Mansion proud.

Hillary rushes to fall into step with me, linking arms and crying lightly. "Okay. So. This is scary, and I think you were right about this being a very bad thing. When we heard you all screaming, I tried to come see if you were okay, but the guards wouldn't let us leave the room."

"I know," I say quickly. "They tried to keep us in there, but the fight was too intense. They had to try to help, so everyone stopped caring about us."

"Fight? The vampires are *fighting*?" she asks, horrified.

I wince. "Killing each other, Hil. They're *killing* each other."

"Oh my God. Over what?"

"Women, I assume. But I don't know. It doesn't matter anymore. What matters is finding a way out of here and quick. Cal told me where to go to get safe."

"If the vampires are so bad, how do you know you can trust him?" she questions reasonably as we keep running, the pack of half-nakedness following behind us.

"Because I just…*can*," I say with only conviction in my voice. "Trust me. There's so much I have to tell you, but for now, just know we can. And if you can't do that right now, do it for the other reason. Because we're shit out of other options."

"Got it." She nods.

Cutting the chitchat and focusing on the objective, Hillary and I lead the group of women on a wild, weaving run through fifteen long halls of distinguished portraits and full bookshelves.

Discouragement grows as we turn the group around for the fifth time in a row, coming to yet another dead end.

"*Shit.*" Fighting dejection, I breathe hard, trying to hold oxygen in my lungs.

"Romy?" a woman in all black suddenly asks, her appearance from the hall at my side both confusing and relieving me all at once. She's not one of the women to be auctioned—she's covered in way too much material.

"Yeah?" I ask.

"I'm Kylie." She hooks a thumb over her shoulder to another beautiful woman behind her. "And this is Blair. We're Rook's and Kane's mates."

"Mates?" Hillary asks, startling me from right behind.

I nod. "Cal's brothers' mates. And…I'm Cal's."

"Holy shit, you're joking! Way to bury the lede, Romy!"

"Come on," Blair interrupts. "Door's this way. More gofers will be here soon, so we have to move now."

Cupping my hands around my mouth, I yell to the women

who've scattered now, frantically searching every room on the hall. "Ladies! Over here! Come on! The door's this way."

A game of telephone transpires as they work to pass on the message, and Hillary and I wait at the entrance to the hall, counting until we're sure all the women have made it through.

Out on the lawn, we move in the low light of the still-rising moon in a cluster like a bunch of scantily clad geese.

"I swear," I mutter to Kylie, Blair, and Hillary, having sprinted back up to the front of the group after we were sure everyone was out. "If this weren't so terrifying, it'd be a hell of a story to make fun of. I don't even want to think about what it's going to look like when we make it to the road."

"We have a bus waiting with a hundred sets of sweats inside," Blair says with a laugh. "Kane and Rook procured it earlier today on Cal's orders."

"Thank God," I manage with a laugh as we finally make it to the tree line Cal told me would be here.

And just like he said, the light beckons in the distance. It'll still be a long trek in the pitch dark in six-inch heels or bare feet— but the nightmare is almost over.

I can see the end of the tunnel.

And the future with Cal on the other side of it sure looks bright.

As long as he makes it out alive...

24

Cal

E'RE AT A BREAKING POINT.

More than a hundred vampires are dead, including Narris and the rest of the Council, and every gofer sent as backup, all at our hands. For a guy who doesn't tire, I'm fucking exhausted.

Five men joined us in our fight, along with Julian, and for that, we're grateful. I'm not sure we would have been able to maintain our edge without them, and it's certainly a moral victory as far as my faith in our species as a whole goes.

They came here to Selection as a matter of course, but when faced with a choice between right and wrong, they picked the correct side of history. I don't know what this will mean for them, their futures, and their family's bloodlines, but it's not my job to care.

Right now, all I care about is this standoff between the Wraths and the Slaters.

And how only one set of brothers is making it out of this alive.

Rook shoves Nathanial back, but when Cassian catches Kane

off guard, he manages to shove my middle brother to the floor hard.

Before I can stop it, my fucking piece-of-shit father Cassian uses Kane's position to his advantage, jumping on him instantly. He presses his knee to Kane's throat and locks his hand at his jaw hard enough to force his head back at an angle that's seconds away from snapping.

Fuck!

Rook's chest heaves as he and his father Nathanial stand two feet on either side of them.

Ronan is hurt but alive, his leg badly mangled where he lies in front of Lucian. Given enough time, he'd heal. But I'm afraid, if I have anything to say about it, he doesn't have much time left at all.

"Let him go or else I will fucking murder you!" Rook bellows.

"Kill him," Nathanial encourages.

"If you let them kill my brother, Lucian, it will be the end of you," I spit.

Lucian is standing behind the pulpit with his hand wrapped around the edge of the wood. I'm not stupid enough to think Lucian will be easy to kill. I know there's a very real possibility I won't be able to. His abilities are so far superior to anything I've ever fought before.

But I will do whatever I have to fucking do for my brothers.

"Lucian, I said kill him!" Nathanial calls again, surprising me.

I expected his directive was for my father, to kill Kane, but evidently, it's not.

Instead, it's a plea for a cheat—for their precious eldest brother to use his powers to earn the advantage. "Do some of that voodoo shit and end these fuckers, Luc!" Nathanial demands.

Having experienced Lucian's pain-rendering firsthand, I brace myself for the feeling with a tightening of my abdomen. I know it'll bring me to my knees, and if he wishes, choke the life out of me completely.

But it never comes.

Nathanial grabs his chest suddenly, backing away long enough for Rook to catch Cassian off guard and take back control. He charges, freeing Kane, and then besting Cassian with a quick and deadly snap of his neck.

One Wrath—my father—is dead.

Three more to go.

"Why, thank you, Rook," Lucian says inexplicably, rounding the pulpit and walking slowly toward Nathanial.

I know Nathanial is in pain, and I know I'm not, but the precious two seconds it's taken for so much to occur haven't left time for my mind to catch up. Our bodies are simply too fast.

"Thank you?" Rook questions, his chest still heaving with rage, and confusion finding footing for him too.

"Yes," Lucian agrees simply. "For doing some of my work for me."

"What the fuck are you talking about?" Kane asks, on his feet now and completely untrusting of Lucian's intentions. I don't blame him. Since the moment Lucian Wrath showed up at our cabin in Connecticut, nothing he's done has gone according to plan.

"Yeah, Lucian. What the fuck?" Nathanial chokes out, still clutching his chest in pain. "What's going on? Why are you doing this to *me*? Kill them already!"

Lucian's calm is rooted in ruthlessness as he stalks his own brother. "What's going on, Nathanial, is a man playing the long game of revenge."

Nathanial groans, and Lucian's smile grows.

"You see, nearly thirty years ago, I came to my first Selection and fell uproariously in love with a woman of unmatched beauty and kindness. I didn't agree with the methods of the Council or the tradition of the auction, but for lack of options, thanks to Father, I decided that I would allow myself the pleasure of the woman of my dreams. Bought, of course, because that's how these things work, but I didn't mind the idea of putting in the work anyway. Of delaying the bonding and courting her instead. I wanted to show her care. Love. The life of luxury we're *so good* at promising."

"Lucian," Nathanial begs, dropping to the floor now, the pain is so intense.

"But I lost that bid, didn't I, brother?" Lucian questions before kicking Nathanial in the chin, sending him rolling as spit flies to the floor in front of him.

Ronan screams in protest or pain, I can't tell which, but with one flick of his hand, Lucian sends him to his own bout of spine-rending agony.

"I lost that bid to *you*, Nathanial," Lucian continues. "You took the woman I loved out from under my nose, and you ruined her. You abused. You tortured. You depleted. And when that wasn't enough, you shared her *with our brothers.*"

"Fuck you," Nathanial grits out. "That whore got what she deserved."

With a sickening crunch, Lucian kicks him again, laying him flat out with a groan.

Squatting, Lucian hovers over his brother, the only sound

the clicking whisper of a tsk. "Now, now. Don't rush me along. I've been waiting thirty years for this."

"Lucian," Nathanial cries, none of the cockiness he's carried for the past three days left in his voice. He's faceup, weak, and in intense agony from his own brother's specialty.

And just like that, it all makes sense.

Why Lucian brought us here to do the groundwork he couldn't do himself. Why he brought me to my brothers and unlocked the door.

Why he waited until the middle of the auction to announce my mating—an event I'm now certain he facilitated all along.

It's no coincidence that Romy ended up with the room at the end of the hall out of a hundred other women, the only room with a window to the outside.

It's no coincidence that this place, the chosen location for this year's Selection, is actually Lucian's house—a choice he, no doubt, used his position on the Council to lobby for. He wanted the high ground, the tools, and the army to execute a plan he's had for decades.

A plan he strategized for the sole purpose of avenging *our mother*. The woman he lost in the first bid before choosing his mate Helenna in the second.

He gave her the life he would have given our mother and loved her gently, all while our mother suffered. Helenna dying last year must have been his breaking point.

Bottom line, Lucian played me.

He played all of us, and he did it with selfish focus. If we were casualties of the game, so be it. But his endgame was the same as ours all along.

Crumble the Council. Buck the tradition. Make the evil men pay.

It's why Kane's had such a hard time with the muddiness of his intention, and it's why I've been struggling to get a read on him from day one. Lucian's a shield, but he picked and chose the moments he kept from me, silencing the conversation he had with Narris in the selection room for the purpose of giving me a reminder of the reason I had to fight in front of all the men so there'd be as much chaos as possible.

He didn't stop me from listening any other time, something I now know was intentional.

He knew I was prepared to do what was necessary. Quite possibly, he knew the way my brothers and I were raised prepared us more than anyone else. Group homes. Fosters. Raising ourselves and fighting for everything we had.

This man had a *plan*. And decided we were the ones to help him execute it.

"Lucian," Nathanial cries again, sounding like a damn baby as the agony takes on new heights. "Brother, please."

"You, Nathanial, are no brother of mine," Lucian spits. "I'm disgusted by your blatant disregard for not only Naomi, but every other human woman who's followed in her wake."

Naomi. Our mother's name was Naomi.

My chest surges with pain and pride and a lifetime of longing. I didn't realize how much her absence meant through the day-to-day, but I can see now it's what made us the way we are.

The constant drive to live up to the men she'd want us to be—the need to stop what happened to her from happening to other women.

Cal? Romy asks, obviously feeling my despair dancing across her own skin.

I'm okay, my love. Are you safe?

Yes. We just got on the bus and got dressed.

Good. I'll see you soon.

Reassured that the most important part of our plan has come together, I interject myself into my uncle's game.

"How long did he wait before he abused her, Lucian? Had the bond even settled?"

"No, Calloway," he responds. "It's safe to say Nathanial saw your mother as nothing more than a possession from the start."

Lucian grabs Nathanial by the chin one final time, his fingers digging into the flesh and melting it right there. Bone exposes and everything else vaporizes just like what he did to Lexor in the cabin.

Except this time, Nathanial is still alive and suffering. His cries are loud and agonized as Lucian spits directly in his eye.

"Rot in hell, brother. For Naomi. For all of them. Not a soul on this earth will miss you."

Nathanial crumples to the floor, his body half gone in vapored mist.

And Ronan whimpers, painfully awaiting a similar fate, but Lucian is evidently done with theatrics. With one wave of his hand, Ronan expires.

Lucian looks slightly weakened by the exertion, moving slowly to one of the remaining chairs and sinking down into it.

I look back at Julian and the other men who've joined us, my jaw tight and my threats anything but empty. "We thank you for fighting with us. But make no mistake, if you betray us and our purpose, we will kill you too."

They nod, their eyes wide and humbled not just by me, I suspect, but by the spectacular display of Lucian's speech and brotherly revenge.

"Find your fated mates and treat them well," Rook adds. "You'll be surprised how much better it will be to nourish what nature has given you. To extend fate's destiny with your line."

"Pack your things and leave!" Lucian says then, his voice a command none of them dares challenge. They leave the room in a blur of motion.

I round the chair to stand in front of Lucian, not with kindness, but with demands. I can appreciate and sympathize with his story, and today, he did the right thing. But there is right to be done. Penance to be paid.

Even at the threat of his certain overpowerment, I will not bow down. "I want your assurances that this is the end, Lucian. No more Selections. No more women forced into anything other than a bond of their destiny."

"My Calloway." He shakes his head, his mouth upturned in a proud smile. "I knew you were the one. In fact, I knew the Slaters were the only way." He sighs. "Yes, as the de facto head of the Elite Council, I appoint the three of you as my replacements. You, Rook, and Kane are in charge now. I vow it."

"Three blue-collar guys…head of the elite state. I'm sure everyone will love that," Rook grumbles. "That's not fucking happening, Lucian."

Lucian just chuckles. "Of course, there will be pushback, Rook. And there will likely be other groups that seek to supersede you. As you know, our rule extends only along the East Coast. Globally, there are twenty-five other Councils that won't be keen to bend to your rules."

"We've fought our fight," Kane argues. "The rest will be up to someone else."

Lucian's glowing green eyes flick between us, as if he already knows that's not how it ends. As if he's certain this is something we can't say no to.

My jaw sharpens. *I refuse to let myself fall victim to biting off more than I can chew. And I'm sure as shit not unknowingly stepping into another war just because Lucian has put us in an unwinnable situation.*

"And these women?" I ask. "What will they do?"

Lucian pushes to standing, cracking his neck back and forth while a quiet exhale leaves his throat like he's already tired of our answer.

"Come," he says, motioning for us to follow. "Let's discuss it in my office."

25

ROMY

RIGHT LIGHTS SHINE FROM THE GATE AS IT OPENS in front of us, and the bus pulls into a long, packed gravel drive. I shield my eyes against the onslaught of pupil-piercing brightness as the bus lets off the airbrakes and moves once again, standing from my seat and moving to the front.

My feet are bloody from running in heels for the first mile, and the soles, cracked from running the second when I took them off. My hair is disheveled and my makeup a mess, and the scrape on my palm from the fall I took climbing through the thorns at the edge of the road still stings.

But when the light fades and settles, the last sight I'd ever expect comes into view.

I swear, this is a drive I've made before.

A drive that brought me to hell three days ago.

A drive that ends at the place from which we just escaped.

The stonework is the same color and texture, and the still, quiet of fog over the grounds sends an eerie shiver down my spine.

It can't be. It can't.

Tears prick my eyes as overwhelm slams into me.

For some reason, instead of taking us to a secure location far away, the savior bus I was so sure of has brought us right back to the place we've spent the last two hours running away from, and who knows what monsters lurk.

The Elite Council? Punishment for our escape?

"What the hell is going on?" one of the other girls asks, her voice shrill and panicked, watching as we round the circle and the palatial front staircase comes into view. As the other women take notice, the volume of palpable fear on the bus only grows.

"Why are we back here?" Hillary questions, devolving almost immediately into tears. "I thought you said we were going somewhere safe!" she accuses then, turning directly to Blair and Kylie.

She put her trust in the three of us—all these women did. It's monumental when I think about how impossible it seemed at the start. And now, it looks as though we've betrayed them.

"If we're back here, it's for a reason. Kane will have a reason," Blair argues confidently. "Trust me, I've been through some absolutely wild shit with them that I thought was the end of the world, and I know now how necessary it all was."

"Rook, too," Kylie agrees. "He would never put any of us back in danger. He's put his life on the line too many times to save mine."

They do their best to set everyone's nerves at ease, but it's a losing battle with a hundred hysterical women. I don't bother with my own anecdote about Cal literally snapping a man's neck to save me earlier, because with emotions this high, it won't do any good.

"Yeah, sure, if either of them is still alive," a woman named Whitney hisses. "Maybe your precious mates lost the fight. Did you ever think of that?"

Unfortunately, I didn't. In my mind, there was no possibility that Cal could lose. Fate, surely, wouldn't give me the biggest gift of my life, just to rip it away before we ever got started.

Would it?

As chaos builds, I make my way to the front windshield and grab on to the handle to open the door. As soon as we come to a stop, I pull it and hit the ground running.

My feet are already torn apart—they can't get any worse. And if Cal is somehow dead without my knowing, I'd rather be dead myself anyway. It doesn't matter what dangers face me. Not knowing if Cal is alive or not is worse.

I haven't been able to reach him since we made it to the bus, but I told myself it was just the distance. That our communication somehow lost signal like a walkie-freaking-talkie.

My knees shake and my hips jolt as I take the stairs two at a time despite a raging pain in my feet. As the door opens and Lucian appears at the threshold, I slide to a stop, a cry sticking precariously in my throat.

No. No!

His eyes are keen as ever as he recognizes me, a small, sad smile lifting the corners of his mouth.

"Romy, my dear—"

"Cal!" I yell, daring to cut him off, no matter the risk. "Where's Cal?"

He nods. "Don't worry—"

"Romy!" Cal's yell is guttural as he bursts through the door and pulls me into his arms.

I shake and cry, burying my face in his neck as he gathers me as close as he can. "Shh, it's okay. Shh."

"I couldn't get in touch with you, and then when we got

back here, I thought…" My sniffles make it nearly impossible to continue.

Lucian, though not part of our conversation at all, chimes in. "I'm afraid that's my fault, and I apologize. When I get worked up, my shielding runs a little overactive. I was likely blocking you from each other unintentionally."

Rook and Kylie and Kane and Blair reunite on the steps just below us, and while I'm on edge, the three Slater brothers seem to be mostly at ease. I don't fully understand it—how they're so calm with Lucian right here talking about shielding us from communicating, but they are.

Cal's face softens in understanding when I jerk my head toward the old, evil vampire in question. "Turns out, he's on our side."

My eyes narrow, and he laughs. "I know, we were skeptical too. But Kane confirmed. His intention is pure."

"But he's a shield," I argue. "I read something about shields—"

Lucian interrupts my rant with a laugh. "What a smart, tough woman you've been given, Calloway. Cherish her."

Cal nods. "I will."

"Ladies," Lucian calls, addressing the crowd of women who've now amassed at the bottom of the grand stairs. "I want to thank you for your unyielding patience and apologize for the atrocities you've been subjected to while here. I know this is what some of you were raised to expect, but no woman should have to forfeit her autonomy for the chance at a better life for her family. Period."

He pauses briefly for a roll of chatter to die down before he goes on. "You have a choice. The first one: you can leave now, with all your belongings and a sworn vow of no further interference in your lives. Your families will still receive the dowry they were promised, and it'll be your preference whether you find companionship in a vampire of any stature, a human, or no one at all. The second: if you want help finding a mate, whether destined or courted, of vampire descent, you'll be given it. I will be vacating these grounds and returning to the Cape, but anyone who chooses to stay will be welcome. You'll be serviced by a fully female staff and assisted with job opportunities in the area if you wish."

"The point, I suppose, is that the choice is yours," Lucian continues. "For the first time in two hundred years, you are invited to be the architects of your own lives. Your new Elite Council—who've elected to be known only as *The Council* now—will fight for it. They've proven that today."

He gestures with a wide arm, opening it to Rook and Kane and Cal.

I stare up at Cal with wide eyes, and he looks down at me with a little grin.

"Oh, so, by the way…" he whispers. "Something worth noting—I'm in charge now."

The bomb hasn't even fully detonated before he's stepping slightly away to join his brothers.

"Ladies, meet your new Council," Lucian announces. "The Slater brothers. Rook, Kane, and Calloway. I assure you, with them at the helm, you're in good hands."

CAL

WITH GENTLE HANDS, I UNWRAP THE now-cooling cloth from Romy's feet and replace it with another as she lies back on the bed upstairs—the one we completed our mating in just last night.

I wanted to leave and take her to a hotel, but when Hillary, Abigail, and fifty percent of the other women decided to stay at Lucian's mansion, Romy said she couldn't in good conscience go anywhere.

I, of course, understood the feeling.

The differences, however, are noticeable. The armoire is permanently moved and the shade lifted, and bright moonlight spills across the floor. Happy gabbing and consorting among the women is audible from the hall as they move from one room to the other, playing music and making calls on their newly returned phones.

Kylie, Rook, Kane, and Blair now occupy rooms here in the main house, and dinner tonight was shared and made with love by the whole group. Though, we vampires didn't do any of the actual eating.

Contact with the outside world is restored, autonomy is back, and the vibes within this old, moody house are charging forward in a steep ascent.

It'll take time for everything to be sorted entirely, and I'm not exactly looking forward to my new role as some kind of governmental figure, but I am thrilled to have the chance to be in control of my own life.

For Romy and Blair and Kylie and their relatives and friends to be at the helm of theirs.

Still, the condition of Romy's feet burns in my chest, and the fight she was left to put up on her own as they ran for their lives courses through me in ways only a mated vampire could understand.

It's my job to protect her. My job to provide care and ease and love. And tonight, I let her down.

"Hey," she says, her voice soft as I spiral through thoughts of could'ves and would'ves on repeat. "It's no big deal. I'm okay. You're okay. Your brothers are okay, and so are all the women. I'd say that's a pretty good outcome."

I shake my head, applying an extra towel to the outside of her new dressing. "Never again will you know the fear you had here. Never again will you have to go it alone."

She laughs, and my head jerks up from her feet to meet her eyes.

They shine with unshed tears and the kind of consideration I never dreamed I would have from someone. It's special. Unspeakable, even. "Cal, I wasn't alone today. Sure, I was running through some woods while you were here fighting, but I carried you with me the whole way. When I reached out, you answered."

She shakes her head, and a small smile covers her pretty mouth.

"In the middle of, like, an epic battle, you were answering me." She snorts. "Do you know how many men say they can't answer a text during a simple meeting in the human sphere? How they don't have time for a call between work and the gym?"

"It doesn't scare you that I did what I did today? Scare you that I'm capable of it?"

Romy's lips are soft as she purses them toward me. "That you killed for me after saying very early on that you would kill for me?" She sighs. "No. You said what you meant, and now I know I can count on your word."

Climbing her body carefully, I kiss every inch of skin left exposed by her small shorts and cropped tank top. I create a trail from her legs to her stomach to her chest, and I don't stop until I make it to her mouth.

"Who knew this outfit my mom forced me to bring would come in handy," she teases in between kisses.

"I know a bonding is much different than a relationship usually is," I say softly, my lips turning up at her amazing ability to find the humor in any of this. "It's lightning-fast and leaves no room for negotiation."

"Cal, let's be honest. Our bond is the slowest in vampire history."

"What?" I tilt my head to the side. "What do you mean?"

"I've been in love with you since I was ten," she answers with a laugh. "Over a decade in the making? We have to have set some kind of world record."

"I love you," I say, kissing her slowly until she wraps her arms around me, and all the noise of this house and my mind fade completely away.

"I love you too, Cal," she gasps, breathless from the kiss in a way that reminds me how precious her humanness is. It's a gift. *She* is a gift.

The greatest of all.

Whatever challenges we face in the future, I will meet them head on. Whatever evil finds us next, I will best.

Whatever should threaten this—my most cherished bond—I will destroy.

I may be considered noble now. A leader of this group of vampires and an official member of the new Council.

But for Romy Spencer, I will always and forever be her *Demolition Man.*

Epilogue

PART ONE

CALLOWAY

One year later

STONE WALLS TOWER OVER US IN THE BACK courtyard of Lucian's Westchester estate as fellow vampires Julian, Norwood, Gregory, Benjamin, Malik, and Wallace take seats on the benches in front of us.

Rook stands his ground in the back, his mind largely preoccupied with Kylie's impending delivery of their first child and his general skepticism of everything otherwise ever-present.

The first year as the new head of the Council for this region has been tumultuous to say the least. Pushback, upset, and questions from the previously classed elite, along with support, excitement, and understanding from everyone else, have kept us much busier than we'd like.

For Rook, that's meant an even grumpier mood at times.

Kane, on the other hand, loves all the fucking drama and attention and being at the helm of socializing.

"Gentlemen," I greet, crossing my arms over my chest and getting down to the business of why I've called the men who fought alongside us in this very mansion last year here in the first place. "I appreciate you coming, and more than that, we appreciate the support you've provided us over the last twelve months of transition. We know there's a long way to go in restoring universal order to the vampires as a whole, but I'm happy to say that the health and vitality of our group is thriving."

All three of our mates are pregnant, the number of fated mate pairings is at an all-time high, and as far as we can tell, there haven't been any ill effects from nature running its own course with the bloodlines.

Holland and some of the other gofers involved in the underground trafficking of women are the biggest thorns in our sides in this region, but while I'd rather they were dead, they're suffering more in their new stature—serving as blue-collar workers in the day-to-day, and for Holland specifically, working as a garbage man. We keep a close eye on them too, just in case.

"We're happy with things this way, Cal," Julian says. "It took a lot of balls to stand up for what was right, but I'm glad you did. As soon as I returned home, I met my mate. It took some courting, but as of six months ago, we're officially bonded." He confirms our success firsthand. "I owe you gratitude, and as such, this meeting felt like the least I could do."

"Same," Malik agrees. "My mate is expecting. We just found out."

"That's great, Mal," Kane congratulates. "Give Whitney my best wishes."

Kane has done a particularly good job in his new role with vampire relations—which isn't much of a surprise, and I've been more inclined to stick to the mechanics and logistics side of things. Rook has handled any disgruntled complaints. However, I'm pretty sure it wasn't a nice meeting like this where he held their hand.

Daily life, however is much the same, just moved to the outskirts of a different city. I'm still working at my newly rebuilt shop, Kane's still repossessing, and Rook still does his route every week. Though, we don't necessarily need the money and tend to put in half the hours we used to.

Our living situation had to change a bit—given how the fucking gofers burned all our shit down—but it's for the best. We rebuilt on the grounds where our cabin is, a compound-style family place. Each of us has our own house now—mine, Rook's, and Kane's. And the actual cabin itself serves as more of a guesthouse for people like Kylie's Gammy and old roommate Alyssa, Blair's sister Bonnie, and Romy's best friend Hillary to come visit.

"Well, if you hadn't guessed already, I brought you here with a larger purpose than just to give my repeated thanks," I continue. "We've invited you here because we need manpower. There's too much to manage for just the three of us, and with all the threats we receive from other groups on the daily, we need to be organized and capable. We'd like the six of you to join us as members of the Council."

"We need the help, and you were the best we could find," Kane adds teasingly, making the group laugh.

"You can take time to think on it," I say. "You don't have to agree now if you're not ready, but—"

"I'm in," Julian cuts me off to agree. "I'd do anything to keep things the way they are now. To keep the sanctity of what you've created here. So, yeah. I'm in."

"Me too," Benjamin agrees.

"Whitney's been telling me I need something to keep me occupied so I stop worrying over her pregnancy so much. This fits the bill nicely," Malik chimes in.

Kane laughs. "Speaking of worrying over pregnancy…" He hooks a thumb toward Rook. "That's why you're looking at a brick wall with this one. Kylie could go any minute."

Rook growls, and I smother a smile. Just like with the kidnappings and the bonding craziness, I know Kane and I will both be eating our words soon when Romy and Blair are close to delivering too. It's biological.

"Norwood, Gregory, Wallace?" I question. "What about you guys?"

Norwood nods. He's the strong, silent type, so I don't take offense at the lack of enthusiasm. If anything, that's as good as seeing him jump up and down.

"It's a cause I'd be proud to die for," Gregory says solemnly, igniting Kane's humor button again.

"Trust me, Greg, we're hoping that doesn't happen."

"Things have been quiet," I agree. "Being prepared is purely precautionary at this point."

"Well, I can't be the only guy to bow out," Wallace finally says with a smile. "Not that I want to be. I'm in. You just tell me what I need to do."

"Fuck!" Rook snaps in an outburst, making all of us jump, it's so unexpected.

"What the hell?" Kane asks, his hands up in a karate-chop position that's so damn comical I can't help but laugh.

"Kylie's in labor!" he yells, but I swear he's already gone in a blur.

Kane holds up a hand before chasing after him, and I'm left to wrap things up.

"Anyway, we appreciate you all. But for now, I guess we're going to have to cut this meeting short."

Julian's smile is genuine as he holds out a hand to shake mine. "Give Rook our best."

I nod. "We'll be in touch. Proud to have you as a part of our cause."

PART TWO

ROOK

One year later

I push through the door of mine and Kylie's house, following the voices carrying from down the hall.

My jaw clenches when I hear Kylie grunt out in pain.

I burst into the spare bedroom, and the scent of sterile medical equipment hits me straight in the face. As parents of an unborn vampire baby, we have to be prepared for birth a little differently from most humans—aka deliver at home with a medical team that knows the deal.

Dr. Howard stands near the hospital bed we had shipped

in just for this occasion, and two nurses move around him with practiced efficiency, but I barely register any of it.

Because all I fucking care about is Kylie.

She's propped up against the pillows with her legs in stirrups. Her hair is damp and clinging to her skin, and her breathing is uneven as another wave of pain rolls through her. She grips the sheets, knuckles white, her whole body tightening against something that won't let go.

I rush over to her without hesitation. My girl is strong. I know that. I've seen it. But this feels different. I don't like it one fucking bit.

"I'm here, baby," I whisper, reaching down to pull her hand into mine.

"Apparently, vampire babies come a lot quicker than human ones." She offers a small smile, and I kiss her sweat-drenched forehead.

"I love you so fucking much."

"I love you too," she whispers through a clenched jaw. "But I'd also love to get our baby out of my body. Otherwise, I might end up as grumpy as you here soon."

Another contraction hits, and her body tenses beneath my hand, her breath catching as pain overtakes her. Immediately, I drag my gaze to the doctor.

"How much longer, Doc?" I ask, my tone leaving no room for anything but a straight answer.

He meets my eyes briefly. "Not too much longer. You're doing great, Kylie."

Kylie moans through another contraction, her small body tensing up in ways that make my chest ache.

"Can't you give her anything for the fucking pain?" I question, anger rising in my throat. "A fucking epidural or something?"

"Unfortunately, it's too late for that," Dr. Howard says, and there's a huge part of me that wants to fucking throttle him.

I'm fine, Rook, Kylie pushes into my mind. *Also, please don't hurt the doctor. I need him to deliver our baby.*

Fuck. I hate seeing you in pain, baby.

"I'm okay," she says out loud, her voice strained but sure.

Her eyes lift to mine, and I hold her gaze for a second longer than necessary, searching for anything that tells me otherwise, but there's nothing to be found.

The next stretch of time blurs into something that feels both too fast and not fast enough. I stay exactly where I am, her hand in mine, my body angled toward her like I can shield her from the worst of it, even though I know I can't.

I watch every shift in her expression, every tightening of her jaw, every breath she pulls in as she pushes through something that would break most people.

But she doesn't break because my Kylie is so fucking strong.

"Okay," Dr. Howard announces with a smile. "Next two contractions, we're going to have our baby."

Kylie nods, already bracing herself, and when the next wave hits, she bears down with everything she has. A sound breaks from her—raw, unfiltered—and it cuts straight through me.

My grip tightens around her hand. "That's it," I murmur, even though I hate every second of this. "You're doing so fucking good, baby. I'm so proud of you."

She exhales sharply, her body trembling as the contraction eases.

"Last one, Kylie," the doctor says. "And your baby will be here."

I lean closer, my forehead nearly brushing hers. "You've got this," I tell her, my voice rougher now. "I've got you."

The next contraction hits, and Kylie pushes again, pushes with everything inside her, and everything inside me goes still.

And then, a cry fills the room.

It's sharp and beautiful and *alive.*

"It's a girl!"

For a second, the words don't fully land.

A girl?

A girl?

My chest tightens as something deeper than instinct settles into place.

After everything that was done by the corrupt elites, no one knew if it would ever be possible again. In the name of power and control and greed, they created so much chaos, caused so much damage. They destroyed the equilibrium of our kind and the noble human bloodlines.

Because of them, there hasn't been a female vampire born in centuries.

And yet, I have a *daughter.*

Our bond established equilibrium again.

All because Kylie's and my bond has a foundation of the three most important factors—I'm elite, Kylie's *blood of the three,* and we're fated mates.

I look down to find a beautiful baby girl with big blue eyes and a head full of dark hair.

The doctor places her—our daughter—gently on Kylie's chest, and the sight of them together hits harder than anything else ever has. The instant mother and daughter are united, our baby girl's cries stop, but her eyes stay open as she gazes up at her mama.

Kylie looks down at our baby girl, tears in her eyes and her expression soft in a way I've never seen before.

Beautiful doesn't come close.

I press a kiss to Kylie's forehead, letting it linger for a second before I shift lower and brush my lips gently against our daughter's head.

She's tiny. She's perfect. She's *ours*.

And something inside me settles in a way I didn't know it could.

"I know what we should name her," Kylie whispers, looking up at me.

"Yeah?"

She glances down at our daughter again, then back up at me. "Naomi."

My mother's name.

For a moment, I can't speak. I just look down at my mate, at our daughter, at the life we created, at everything this means.

Everything it fixes.

Everything it restores.

My throat tightens as I finally find my voice. "Naomi," I say, softer than I've ever said anything in my entire fucking life.

And it fits because that's her name—Naomi, our beautiful daughter.

Movement at the doorway pulls my attention, and Kane and Calloway step in first, followed by their mates Blair and Romy. Gammy comes in behind them, and I can tell by the tears in her eyes she's already emotional.

Everyone who matters is here.

I gaze down at Kylie, leaning in to kiss her again. When I pull back, I rest my forehead against hers, letting myself take it in for just a second.

All of it.

We burned the old, corrupt world of elite vampires and built something new in its place.

And clearly, we got it right.

I look at Kylie and Naomi again.

My fated mate. My daughter.

My entire fucking world.

PART THREE

KANE

Five months later

"Are you guys tired or some shit?" I tease as I skate past one of the guys on Blue Steel.

He shoots a glare in my direction, and I just laugh as I reach out and snag the puck away from his stick, flicking past him with ease and sliding a pass across the ice to Rook.

There's still room for debate on whether my brothers and my building a private hockey rink a few miles away from our compound was a good idea, but I'm in the camp that believes it certainly fucking was.

Every other Thursday, we invite other vampire teams from nearby towns to come play us. And tonight, Blue Steel probably regrets agreeing to this match.

Iron Knights: 6

Blue Steel: 2

The scoreboard flashes above us, and I tap my stick against the ice as I watch the puck slide across it.

"You guys wanna try playing defense, or is this more of a participation situation?" I taunt the biggest dude on Blue Steel's team.

"Shut the fuck up," he spits, and I blow him a kiss.

Calloway skates past me and shoves my shoulder. "How about you cool the taunting, yeah? I mean, you've only scored one fucking goal, bro."

"Quality over quantity," I shoot back easily. "It might only be one goal, but it was the best goal of the night."

Cal rolls his eyes, and Rook doesn't bother with commentary. He just takes the puck clean from one of their guys and sends it my way without looking like he's trying.

I catch it automatically, cutting across the ice, letting them think they've got a shot before I shift my weight and take it.

The puck snaps into the net.

Iron Knights: 7

Blue Steel: 2

"Go, Kane, go!" Blair cheers from the stands. I glance over my shoulder to find her—fully pregnant and ready to deliver any day now—standing on her feet and clapping her hands. "That's my man!"

"Blair, honey!" I call over toward her. "Could you cheer from a sitting-down position?"

She sticks out her tongue at me, but thankfully, she plants her cute, very pregnant butt on the bleachers. It's safe to say, with Blair being pregnant, every protective instinct inside my body is on full alert.

I glide back into position as Blue Steel tries to take another go at us, but just as the puck is pitched across the ice, something hits me full force.

It's not physical, but everything inside me locks up and consumes my focus to the point that I can't register anything else but her.

Blair.

I turn to find her still in the stands, but she's back on her feet and one hand is gripping the railing near the plexi, while the other is pressed low on her stomach. Her face is pale, her breathing uneven—but when her eyes find mine, it's not fear I feel from her.

It's urgency.

And pain.

Blair's in labor.

I'm moving before the thought finishes forming. I skate hard for the edge, not bothering to slow properly before I step off the ice, yanking my helmet free and tossing it behind me. My skates are next after that.

By the time I reach her, I'm in only my socks and she's bracing through another contraction, her body tightening and her breath catching.

"Hey," I say, already reaching for her, my hands gripping her arms gently. "Talk to me."

She huffs out a breath that almost sounds like a laugh. "I think…" She pauses. "I think…" She winces and pants. "My water broke."

And I don't hesitate. I scoop her up in one smooth motion, cradling her as I move toward the arena's exit.

"Kane!" she exclaims. "Put me down!"

"Uh-uh, baby. You're in labor."

"I'm aware." She sighs. "But I don't need you to freaking carry me!"

"Fastest option, baby," I shoot back without regret. "Also, I look good doing it."

She huffs a weak laugh, and I take that as confirmation I made the right call.

The doors slam open when I push through them, the cold air hitting us as I head straight for the Suburban, everything else fading out.

Nothing matters except getting her home.

Nothing matters except making sure Blair and our baby are okay.

"One more push, Blair."

Dr. Howard's voice is steady, but it barely registers over the sound of Blair's breathing and the way her hand tightens around mine. I lean closer, brushing my thumb over her knuckles, grounding her the only way I can.

"You're strong, Blair. So fucking strong. I'm so proud of you."

"I know," she says, and I want to laugh at how my woman can still be so sassy while she's trying to push a baby out of her body.

"Do you also know that I love you?"

She flashes a little smile at me. "Yep. I know that too."

"Good." I press a kiss to her forehead. "Because I do love you. So fucking much."

"That's really great, Kane, but can we focus on me right now? I'm kind of in the middle of something here."

"Right, right." I grin at her and press one final kiss to her forehead.

Another contraction hits, stronger than the last, and she bears down with everything she has. I feel it in the way her body tenses, in the way her grip tightens, in the way the entire room seems to hold its breath with her.

She pushes and pushes and pushes.

And then, the sounds of our baby's first cries fill my ears.

"It's a girl!" Dr. Howard exclaims.

A girl. Another Slater girl.

Our girl.

They place her on Blair's chest, and I don't think I've ever seen anything as stunning as the look on Blair's face when she sees our daughter.

"Oh my goodness, you're so beautiful," Blair whispers to our baby. "The most beautiful girl in the whole wide world."

I lean in slowly, pressing a kiss to Blair's temple. "I love you. I'm so proud of you."

She looks up at me. "I love you too. So, so, so much."

Silence settles between us as we both just gaze down at our daughter. She's tiny and perfect and has eyes like her mama and light hair like mine.

"She's…" I start, then stop, because there isn't a word that fits how I'm feeling. I let my forehead rest briefly against Blair's. "She's everything."

Blair smiles, her eyes still locked on the baby. "She is."

The room fills after that, not all at once, but slowly, like everyone understands this moment belongs to us first.

Eventually, her parents arrive. They're hesitant at the threshold of our bedroom door before moving closer, their expressions softening the second they see their daughter and their new granddaughter.

The Windsors are no longer in the dark about the old elites. They know about the lies and the deception and the truth behind what they thought they were choosing for Blair.

They know all there is to know, and now, because there is nothing to hide anymore, Blair is able to have a relationship with her family.

Both her mom and dad look overwhelmed with joy and love and all the things grandparents should feel when they meet their grandchild.

Behind them, Blair's sister walks in. But Bonnie doesn't wait to be invited to Blair's bedside like her parents; she just goes.

"Finally!" she exclaims as she carefully wraps her arms around Blair and then presses a soft kiss to our daughter's forehead. "Did it hurt like a motherfucker?"

"Bonnie!" Devney Windsor chastises.

"What?" Bonnie shrugs. "It's a valid question."

"Definitely hurt," Blair answers on a laugh, but then she looks down at our daughter. "But more than worth the pain."

Bonnie smiles down at her new niece. "Hi, little lady. I'm your Aunt Bonnie, and I plan to spoil you in all the ways that will annoy your mom and dad."

Blair snorts. I grin.

"I also brought you something."

"What is it?" Blair asks when Bonnie hands her a gift.

"Just a little something I had made a few months ago."

Blair opens the wrapped box to reveal a handmade doll.

But it's not just any doll. It looks exactly like the vampire dolls Blair got from her parents as a little girl. Just like the vampire doll she says looks like me, only it's the girl version.

Blair goes still for a second, her fingers brushing over it. "But how did you know I was having a girl?"

Bonnie just smiles, a little knowing, a little emotional. "I don't know." She shrugs. "I just did."

The room fills more after that—Rook and Kylie with their baby girl Naomi and Calloway with a smiling but very pregnant Romy.

Later, after everyone has left the room and it's just me and Blair and our daughter, Blair looks up at me with a soft smile on her lips. "I know what we should name her," she says.

"Yeah?"

"Destiny."

I look down at our daughter again, at the tiny life in Blair's arms, at the future we built without even realizing what we were building toward.

Then back at my beautiful Blair.

"Destiny. Our daughter." I lean in, pressing a slow kiss to my mate's lips, letting it mean everything I can't put into words.

When I pull back, I rest my forehead against hers, my hand coming up to cradle the back of our daughter's head.

And somehow, for the first time in a long time, there's nothing left to fight.

Because I already have everything I was meant to find.

PART FOUR
CALLOWAY

Three months later

Romy has never looked more beautiful than she does today. Sweaty, exhausted, and her eyes dancing with the light of a woman about to meet her baby, she finds my gaze and holds it while the doctor tells her to relax.

"Breathe," Dr. Howard coaches. "The next contraction will be here soon, and you need to rest when you can."

"You're doing amazing," I tell her softly, wiping her hair back from her eyes and holding it with my hand. "I'm so proud of you."

Hillary snaps pictures from the other side of the room quietly. Her friendship with Romy has only grown since the night of the auction, and as of a few months ago, she bonded with her own mate. Romy calls Hillary her "homegirl," and that sentiment is clear in the fact that they speak on the phone daily, take frequent trips to the spa, and, by and large, have become family.

As for Romy's parents, they're still not a part of our lives. I've left it up to Romy to make that decision, knowing that the connection to family goes well beyond hurts and disagreements of the past.

Still, the nail in the coffin for Romy came swiftly after we were appointed as the new Council. She reached out to her mother once, intent on changing their relationship and with the hope that she'd be happy for her daughter. All it took was the word "mechanic," though, and her mom hung up the phone.

She didn't leave time for an explanation of my nobility or anything else, and to Romy, that was for the best. If her mother couldn't be happy for her in its purest form, Romy doesn't want her to be happy at all.

As such, she hasn't contacted her since, and today, she's not meeting her grandchild.

It's a shame, but it's my mate's choice, and I respect and understand it.

"I'm tired, Cal," Romy whispers.

"Of course you are, baby." I put a gentle hand on her hair. "But you've got this. She'll be here soon."

"She," she says on a smile that runs my whole world.

"She," I agree. After the other two girls of the next generation made their debut, Romy insisted on going straight to the doctor to find out the sex. I'll admit, I was interested too, if only for the novelty of a whole new female subset of vampires. It's been ages since it happened, and knowing my brothers and I are the reason it changed fills me with pride every day.

Nodding swiftly, she braces as the next contraction takes hold and pulls her knees to her chest. This push is all it takes, and before we know it, the doctor is laying our baby girl on Romy's chest.

"She's here!" the doctor congratulates.

"And she's beautiful," I agree, tears poised in the corners of my eyes. "Just like her mother."

My *daughter*.

"What are we going to name her?" Romy asks, her bottom lip quivering as the doctor lays our daughter on her chest.

And instantly, I know. Three brothers. Three daughters. The power of three.

"Trinity."

Romy smiles up at me, emotion shining in her eyes as she presses a kiss to our baby's head. "Welcome to the world, Trinity."

Sometimes when I look back at everything that's changed, I can hardly believe it.

Us, three blue-collar guys, the new Elite Council. Three female vampire babies in a matter of months with the best human bloodlines in the world. The auction no more and the destiny of the universe restored.

And yet, some things never change.

The Slater brothers will still kill for the women they love.

And they just added three more to the group.

Let's just hope they never have to.

If you accidentally missed a book in the Blue-Collar Vigilante
Vampires Series, check out the entire series here:
https://geni.us/BCVV_Series
If you want to devour another three-book series that's jam-
packed with action, heat, and an enemies-to-lovers romance
that involves a serial killer. Read *Stone Cold Fox* today!

Need EVEN MORE Max Monroe?
Check out our Suggested Reading Order on our website!
www.authormaxmonroe.com/max-monroe-suggested-reading-order

Sign up for our newsletter, and we'll keep you up-to-date on
any news, AND a lot of times, we share fun teasers and excerpts
for our upcoming releases!
www.authormaxmonroe.com/newsletter

Plus, our newsletter is hilarious! Character conversations about
royal babies, parenting woes, embarrassing moments, and shitty
horoscopes are just the beginning! If you're already signed up,
consider sending us a message to tell us how much you love us.
We really like that. ;)

Follow us online here:

Facebook: www.facebook.com/authormaxmonroe

Reader Group: www.facebook.com/
groups/1561640154166388

Twitter: www.twitter.com/authormaxmonroe

Instagram: www.instagram.com/authormaxmonroe

TikTok: vm.tiktok.com/ZMe1jv5kQ/

Goodreads: https://goo.gl/8VUIz2

Acknowledgments

To all the most important people in our lives.

You know who you are.

We couldn't do this without you.

We love you.

To all our reader friends, THANK YOU FOR READING. You're the best.

And last, but certainly not least, to our dream team. The people who surround us and help us turn our words into books. The people who help us reach our readers. The people who support us every step of the way in this industry. Mark Gottlieb, Lisa Hollett, Stacey Blake, Kim Greene, Rick Hambright, Peter Alderweireld, Joanne Cote-Felaccio, Kristina Hassaker, and so many more amazing people, we are forever grateful for you.

XOXO,
Max & Monroe